the daughters of
morrigan

This is a work of fiction. Names, characters, organizations, businesses, places, events and incidents either are the product of the author's imagination or are used fictitiously. Any resemblance to actual persons, living or dead, or actual events is entirely coincidental.

THE DAUGHTERS OF MORRIGAN: Souls Out of Ireland, Book 1
Copyright © 2018 Annie Cosby.

Published by Snowy Wings Publishing
www.snowywingspublishing.com

Cover designed by Regina Wamba of MaeIDesign.com.
Interior by Key of Heart Designs.
Interior graphics designed by Dover Publications, Inc.

All rights reserved. This book or any portion thereof may not be reproduced or used in any manner whatsoever without the express written permission of the author except for the use of brief quotations in a book review.

ISBN: 978-1-948661-00-3

Second Edition.

praise for annie cosby

"A darkly romantic beginning to what promises to be an unusual contemporary YA fantasy series."

- USA Today on *All the Tales We Tell,*
Book One of the Hearts Out of Water Series

"A great mix of YA and Celtic Mythology."

\- Amazon Reviewer on Hearts Out of Water

"This is such an enchanting story! Before reading this, I wasn't very familiar with the Irish tales of selkies, but it was enthralling and refreshing."

\- Amazon Reviewer on Hearts Out of Water

the daughters of morrigan

SOULS OUT OF IRELAND, BOOK ONE

annie cosby

Snowy Wings PUBLISHING

pronunciation guide

Bríd: *breej*

Ríona: *REE-uh-nuh*

Moira: *MOY-ruh*

Faolan: *FWALE-on*

Morrigu: *mor-ig-OO*

Fionn: *fyun*

Medb: *mayve*

"Many paintings were sold, as were the emeralds."

-irish times

arrachtí ón fharraige
MONSTERS FROM THE SEA

moira

It all started with us. Well, as much as anything can be said to start. In truth, it began *again* with us. The day my sister drowned. Nearly. Unfortunately, someone saved her. Or some*thing*, I should say.

Because we were all alone down there on the beach. "Beach" being a relative term in Ireland. There were some sand beaches up near the village, but this was more of a rocky patch between the waves and the field. We were down there alone, like we often were. Me — Moira — and my sisters, Bríd and Ríona, looking for all the world like strangers. And sometimes it felt like we were. Especially that day.

Bríd can be soft as a mouse or mad as a banshee, and so it was as she pranced through the surf, twirling as madly as the waves around her. The wind whipped my hair, streaks of orange dancing in front of my eyes as I frowned at her. She was a tornado of energy on a constant crash course for, well, something, and it often made me feel like a

lifeless block of turf in comparison.

So I did what I did best. I tucked my hair behind my ears and chided her. "*Arah* here, come out of there now — you'll drown yourself!"

"Only you'd worry about that, Moira," she called merrily. "The sea hasn't gotten me in nearly eighteen years, like! Why would it today?"

I didn't know why today, except that there was an unease in my gut and a fierce wind hanging over Connemara. To be fair, that was pretty standard. But it felt all the more menacing today with Dad gone. I didn't like the nights we spent alone when he was away to work. He traveled the country fixing farming equipment, which was a very complicated endeavor that required vast skill and much training. Neither of which Dad had. Because it wasn't actually his job.

It was only the job people thought he had. But when he was away, down into rural Cork, or over in the shiny bright neighborhoods of Dublin, he was actually selling his curios. A biscuit jar that never empties. A stopped clock that only works when it rains. This trip, he was very excited about the prospects for a wheelbarrow that was never heavier than a feather, even when loaded down with stone. These were things certain people would pay very large prices for, and my father knew how to find those people. The problem was, it wasn't always very legal.

Which is why, with each passing day, the knot in my stomach grew bigger. He was never gone longer than a week, and now he'd been gone eight days, with our birthday rapidly approaching. He would never miss our birthday. I wanted nothing more than to scamper back home and wait for his return with my face pressed to the cracked glass of one of the small loop windows that faced the lane.

I glanced over my shoulder, as if to check that the hulking structure on the hill was still there. It'd been there more than five hundred years before us, so it was silly to think it would come down any day now. Still, I longed for my bed, and the fire, and a cup of tea. And the comfort of Dad being home.

But Bríd was in one of her moods, and she can't be stopped when she's in one of her moods. Ríona, Finbar, and I could do nothing but follow in her wake like crows on the wind. Which Finbar is, by the way. Not the wind. But a crow. He perched on a rock near the water, cocking his head at his mistress, who was splashing deeper and deeper into the waves.

Beside me, Ríona heaved a deep sigh, rubbing her goose-pimpled arms as the wind ripped a few curls out of her thick ponytail. Ríona didn't speak. She never had. But I understood her just the same. And that sigh did it. I would speak for the both of us.

"Bríd Doyle, I'm tired, and I want to go home," I called. "I'll go with or without you, but I won't be putting the kettle on for you!" Ignoring her response, I turned back toward the house just as there was a long whinny. My head jerked back around.

A great black horse stepped high in the water toward Bríd. Finbar squawked jealously and flew to his mistress's shoulder.

"What in the world?" I gasped, my gaze automatically snapping to the east field. My old Connemara mare, Bó, stood obediently behind the bawn on the hill, her curious eyes on us.

"And who might you be?" Bríd crooned, stepping toward the strange, hulking horse. It was at least twice the size of Bó. This was no pony.

"Brí—" I called in warning, but her hand was already on the horse's forehead, and it leaned into her touch.

"Here, now, Moira, he's a friendly thing," she said brightly. "Aren't ya?"

But I'd never seen the horse before, and it wasn't so big a village that you saw strange horses romping around the countryside. The horse gave a low neigh and stepped sideways, as if to present his back to Bríd. He was soaking wet, and there were bits of debris and seaweed tangled in his mane. Whomever he belonged to, they hadn't been taking very good care of him.

"He's gentle, see?" Bríd stretched her hand forth as if to climb onto his back.

"Bríd—" I called, a broken record. But she'd already swung deftly onto his broad back, Finbar circling helplessly above her.

The horse sprang into a gallop, first down the shore, Finbar in his wake, then rearing around to run back. Bríd laughed uproariously.

"I think I'll keep him and call him 'Night'!" she yelled as the trio made a great circle around Ríona and me. All we could do was stand helplessly in the surf.

But then something strange happened. The horse pulled a sharp right and ran straight into the waves, toward the open sea.

And he didn't stop.

"Bríd?" I called out.

Her laugh died away. What was she doing? She was going to drown atop that damn beast. This was just like her. Pushing things too far. "Bríd, stop!" I called out. "You're going too deep!"

She looked anxiously over her shoulder as Finbar screeched. He flew after her, continuously buffeted by the wind of the ocean. Something in her face made me pause.

"Stop the horse!" I called out desperately.

"I-I can't!" she yelled. The waves grew bigger by the moment, but the horse didn't waver in his fatal course.

"Then get off! Get off it!"

Ríona splashed haphazardly into the water, tears of fright streaming down her face. I dashed after her, but the waves were too dangerous to go far.

Bríd seemed to struggle, trying to slide off the horse. "I-I'm feckin' caught!" she shrieked, tearing at something in front of her. And on the horse ran.

"Bríd!" I screamed. Her helpless cry urged Ríona and me forward, but we'd never reach them. The water was already up to Bríd's belly, and the horse was almost completely submerged — only its head was visible above the choppy waves. Finbar divebombed the monster's frothing face over and over again.

A howl came from behind us, and Ríona's dog came running down the hill to the shore. We'd left him sleeping soundly at home, but he'd have felt Ríona's anguish from a mile away.

Ahead of me, Ríona froze. Not because her dear Faolan cried in worry for her.

But because Bríd — and the horse — had disappeared underwater. Only the sound of Finbar screeching filled my ears.

"Bríd!" I screamed right along with him.

Ríona dove forward, and Faolan went mad back on shore as I was frozen with the choice of dragging one sister back to shore or joining her in this desperate attempt to save the other.

But I had no time to act — Bríd suddenly resurfaced, tossed above the water by a strong arm. A human arm.

It was attached to a boy.

Swimming swiftly, he propelled Bríd toward the shore as she spluttered and gasped, Finbar circling them with broken coos. Shocked and shaking, I grabbed Ríona's arm as she cried in relief. Finbar gave another piercing shriek, this one rife with solace.

Suddenly, another head popped above the water. The horse, behind my sister and this strange boy, its eyes on fire.

"*Watch out!*" I screamed.

The boy turned and, instead of swimming for his life, he yelled at Bríd, "Go! Get to shore!" before diving toward the monster of a horse. My breath caught in my throat. The horse was frothing at the mouth.

What boy would dive into danger so willingly for a person he didn't know? Because that much I could tell from the few moments I'd glimpsed of his face. He wasn't anyone from the village.

Bríd swam steadily toward us as the boy reached the huffing horse and pummeled it with his bare fist. The horse brought its great head down on the boy's chest. The boy disappeared underwater for a moment, and I cried out. But he reappeared quickly, throwing all his weight at the horse's head.

With a great splash, Bríd stumbled in the surf, and Ríona grabbed her arm to help her up and guide her back to the beach. Faolan protectively circled Ríona's legs, his eyes on the skirmish in the water. "Bríd," I breathed, embracing her, the saltwater soaking into my clothes. But I didn't take my eyes off her savior.

He appeared to be holding his own, as the horse backed away from him, shaking its head angrily.

"W-What is that?" Bríd whispered between chattering teeth as I combed her wet black hair away from her face.

"RUN!"

The call made all three of us turn.

The horse was swimming straight toward us.

"Run!" the boy called again, swimming furiously toward shore. And run we did.

Faolan took up position behind us, growling fiercely as all three of us dashed toward the hill. I had to hold on to Bríd to keep her on her feet. I glanced over my shoulder to find the boy staggering out of the water, likely to save us yet again, when the horse made a sharp turn northward.

He galloped away through the surf. Farther and farther.

I stopped, my shoulders heaving, and my sisters followed suit. The creature didn't stop, just ran madly on, like we were the predators.

The boy, seaweed tangled in his hair like a strange sea monster, stood barefoot on the pebbled shore, watching the horse retreat. Just like that, he'd conquered that monstrous horse. He'd saved all of our lives. Once the horse was out of sight, the boy looked around, as though confused, and then his eyes landed on us.

I hesitated, unsure what we owed this boy who'd saved my sister's life, but Bríd pushed right past me, rushing to his side. "Feck, are you okay?" she asked breathlessly.

He hesitated by the water, his eyes darting around a bit unusually.

He wore pants much too big for him and a plaid shirt like the ones Dad always wore. He looked quite lost. And when his eyes lit on Faolan, he blanched. Faolan was a dear sweet thing, but you wouldn't know that from looking at him. He was a wolf to the untrained eye. And he'd apparently rendered our savior speechless.

"You … You saved me!" Bríd cried, breaking the silence. She stepped forward and threw her arms around him. Ríona and I hung back, awkward and shaky, while Finbar swooped around the boy's head.

The boy stiffened, clearly uncomfortable, and I didn't blame him. Finbar was harmless enough, but I knew others weren't quite so used to sharing close quarters with a wild bird. When she released her savior, Bríd grabbed his arms, her knuckles white.

"Who are you?" she asked. "You're not from around here. What's your name?"

The stranger glanced at us and gulped, his eyes shifting restlessly from shore to water. It looked almost like he had to … think about his answer to the question. I had a feeling that, for the first time in any of our lives, we weren't the strangest people on this beach.

"I'm Bríd," she said. "What's your name?"

He hesitated again. When he finally spoke, he said, "Aidan."

He said it strangely, his accent hard and clear. I watched his eyes go from Finbar, who stood protectively on Bríd's shoulder, to Faolan at Ríona's side. What a circus we must have looked.

"I can't thank you enough, Aidan," Bríd said, and the sentiment had none of her usual flirtatious energy. She was shaken. As she should've been. It was her antics that had gotten us into this mess.

"Will you come inside?" She gestured back toward the hill. "You're sopping wet."

"No, no," he said quickly, glancing around us. "Just, uh, get inside. It's going to storm."

Ríona and I looked at the clear sky. The wind was fierce, but there wasn't a speck of cloud in the wide blue canvas. When I looked back to earth, the boy was hustling away down the beach. Away from the village.

"What on Earth?" I murmured.

"I don't know," Bríd replied, watching his retreating form. "But I am dead lucky he was around."

"Lucky! Lucky!" Finbar mimicked his favorite voice.

"I'm glad you know that," I said crossly. "Come. Let's get you inside." I slipped my arm around the soaking waist of Bríd's dress and tugged her toward the hill, her eyes still on the strange boy walking away down the beach.

bronntanais an caisleán
GIFTS OF THE CASTLE

moira

You would have been forgiven for thinking there was nothing but a ruin on the west side of the rustyback hill. Because you'd have been partly right. There was a ruin on the west side of the rustyback hill, but it was called Bunrowan Castle, and we lived there. Though "castle" is a bit of a misleading term, to be fair.

And of course there was not "only" a ruin on the rustyback hill. There were also three girls, one pony, one dog, one crow, and one man — when he could be trusted not to run off across the country.

Dad had bought the ruins of Bunrowan off the county council before we were born. It had been our mother's dream to fix it up proper, like in its glory days, minus a few of the less useful aspects — like the chapel to the old gods and the *oubliette*. But they hadn't gotten round to it, since money wasn't stretching quite as far as it used to in those years after we were born. And when Mam died, I suppose

everything sort of stagnated. Dad, the castle — everything but us. We shot up like weeds in a crumbled old edifice that only wanted to be left to fall to its knees and sink into the ground for good.

But we wouldn't let it. We couldn't let it. It was the only thing we had, apart from each other.

That fateful day, we scurried between the Whitethorn and Blackthorn trees flanking the path, across the tiny bridge over the Killeen River, through the front door and inside the comfort of home. Bríd went straight for the stairs, shivering in her soaked clothes, and I closed the door gently behind me. There was no slamming of doors around here. Bríd had done that only once, and now her room had no door at all.

Still shaking, I slipped out of my wet boots as Ríona stooped to clean up Faolan. We kept our shoes in a big jumble by the door, and Ríona even had an old rag of a handkerchief hanging from a nail beside the door that she used to wipe Faolan's feet every time he came inside. But it was a farce of gentility. Of course we had rugs scattered about the stone floor of the castle — otherwise, it was cold enough to freeze your feet right off you in the mornings — but the rugs were threadbare and torn, beyond any sort of respect to be paid like taking off shoes or wiping the dog's feet. Still, we paid them that respect anyway. Only Bríd was known to stomp inside in her boots, mud flying, when she was in some huff or another.

Once Faolan was decent, Ríona slipped off her own shoes, followed me to the kitchen, and slumped down in a chair at the table, her head in her hands. Curling up beside the stove, Faolan cocked his head at her. Ríona felt things keenly; sometimes I thought all the more for not being able to express her thoughts aloud. She had perfect hearing, but she hadn't spoken a day in her life. Rubbing her back as I passed her, I went to the little fridge wedged between the wall and the old stove. There was a chill to the air, and I realized the fire must have gone out while we'd been down by the sea. Goosebumps went up and down my arms as I opened the fridge to make sure we had milk. I didn't know how to calm my sisters with anything but a hot cuppa. The kettle was the most modern thing in the kitchen, but for the fridge, which was still older than us. And currently bare. Which it often was, whether Dad was there or not.

"We need to go to the market." I sighed, glancing out the window at the sky foretold to become stormy by the strange boy by the sea.

Who was he? And where had he come from? He wasn't from the village, I knew that much. It wasn't easy to stay mysterious and aloof in a place like this. I knew because Dad had been trying since the day we'd been born. We would have to ask around about any Aidans who might have been new to the place. Despite his heroic deed, it was unsettling that he'd been hanging around the sea so close to the rustyback. Especially when we'd been alone.

A chill went up my spine.

Ríona reached for the old biscuit tin in the middle of the kitchen table. That was where Dad kept all his cash, but the supply was dwindling now that he'd been gone so long. She dug around inside and came up with a handful of coins.

"It'll do," I said, resigned. "But let's hope he's back soon." It would be enough to put together jollof rice or something simple for dinner. But it wouldn't last us forever.

Bríd came down the stairs in a fresh T-shirt and jeans, her wet clothes in her arms and Finbar preening on her shoulder. "What's for dinner? Nearly dying has me famished," she said, lying dramatically across the overstuffed velvet chair beside the stove.

Well, it seems she's recovered from the shock quite nicely, I thought darkly. But it was a bit harsh of me. I knew Bríd would be trying hard to distract us from the stressful day.

"We haven't anything to eat," I said, taking her wet clothes from her. "I'll put these out on the line with Dad's things, and then we'll have to go to the market." Earlier, I'd gone poking around Dad's room for change and found only piles of dirty laundry left sitting there all the time he'd been gone. It was clean and hanging out to dry now, but we were still broke.

"Do you think that's ... wise?" For just a second, Bríd's mask slipped, and I saw the fear behind her eyes.

"Arah, we can stay here and starve, or we go out there and see if the village has been taken over by a roving band of those monsters." My words were full of confidence, but I didn't feel it. It was meant only to assure Bríd. It worked.

"Mmm, do you think Brian Brennan will be around the place?" she asked, twirling her hair, though her eyes were still a little dulled. She was trying to pretend everything was normal. I would do the same. Because we had no other choice. "He's an absolute dote, and I was an absolute witch to him last week. He'll be clamoring for more, j'know?"

God, did I know. There was nothing Bríd liked more than playing games with the lads in the village, and it seemed there was nothing the lads liked more, either. It had always been like that. Bríd drew attention.

And there were times I envied her beauty and lamented our not being identical. But, when my jealousy abated, I always wondered: did it not grow trying, always being looked at?

"Speaking of dotes," Bríd said slowly, the mirth evaporating from her eyes, "who do you think that boy was? *Aidan*. Where'd he come from, like? He just appeared out of nowhere. Out of the ocean! Moira ... Ríona ... What ... What do ye think that *thing* was? That-That *horse*?"

"I don't know," I murmured uneasily. The certainty with which that horse had galloped for the open waves sent shivers down my spine. Ríona gave a little whimper. She jumped to her feet and stalked toward the window, putting her back to us. But I saw how her tall frame shook.

"I couldn't get off its back," Bríd whispered, her gaze fixed on the window, but I was sure she wasn't seeing anything at all. "It was like I was ... stuck. Tangled. Tangled in its wet, slimy mane. I just couldn't get off."

"Brí, do you have any money?" I asked abruptly. These were things too spooky to contemplate. Especially when Dad was gone. "We've scarcely got enough for a proper dinner."

"No," she said, sighing as she seemed to snap back to reality. "I'm broke."

"Aren't you always when it comes to needing it?" I murmured.

Ríona nudged my elbow, and I turned to find her holding a little green plant potted in a chipped ceramic pot.

I looked from her to the plant. It had been sitting on the ledge above the kitchen sink for longer than I could remember, but that was about all I knew of it. It wasn't much to look at, scraggly and turning brown in places, so I couldn't see why she was showing it to me now.

"What is it?" I asked her, and she pointed to the soil at the plant's base. Poking half out of the soil, tangled in feeble roots, was a shiny coin.

"What in the … ?" I breathed.

Bríd dashed over to us. "What is it?"

Ríona dug her finger into the soil and pried the coin free with a little snap.

A plant that grew money? Did Dad know about this? Surely not. Otherwise, he'd have taken it with him. It would have gotten a huge price with the people he knew. Or he'd have kept it for a slow investment. Either way, he would have mentioned it. New curiosities were popping up around the castle all the time. This must have been a recent development.

"It's growing feckin' pounds," Bríd grumbled, huffing back to the table.

Wrong, Ríona signed in ISL.

Indeed, it wasn't a British pound, but the dirty coin in Ríona's palm was nearly as useless to us. It bore the horse of the old Irish half crown, already long out of circulation by the time Ireland had started using the euro before we were born.

"That would be just our luck, j'know?" Bríd went on. "What's the point of a magic castle if it doesn't know what century it is?"

I rubbed the coin clean anyway, meeting Ríona's eyes over the little plant's delicate shoots. She took the piece from me and pocketed it, her eyes sparkling. Of anyone in the family, Ríona liked the castle's magic best. And to be sure, it was a miracle, but the kind of miracle that only sort of helps in any way. A broken mug that repaired itself while you slept and an umbrella that could stop the rain on an entire lane. Nice to have, of course. But nothing we could predict or control. Nothing to keep food in the fridge or make Dad smile more.

Rumors of odd things happening on the rustyback hill had always circulated throughout Connemara, but nobody knew the half of what went on in our home. And they never would, if we had anything to say about it. That was why Dad traveled far away to sell the curios that kept us fed and clothed. He was intensely private. But that didn't stop people from whispering about us at the market and questioning Dad's mental fitness — and whether he should've been trusted to raise three children alone.

"Well, let's go," I said, heading for the door, pausing only a moment to glance out the window. "Before that storm foretold by Bríd's savior boy hits."

Outside, the sky was mockingly bright and clear. But it wasn't the sky I kept glancing at. It was the area down near the water that I wanted to make sure was empty. Empty of creatures. The wind pushed us across the east field toward the road into the village, but I fought against it to climb atop the crumbling curtain wall and call Bó to me. It would make me feel better to see her, touch her. She came cantering over, eager to see me, and I felt a pang of guilt that I didn't have anything to give her for a special treat. She had all the grass and hay a girl could want, and total run of the place, fields and bailey alike, but I loved to spoil her.

She nipped at my hand and snorted angrily when she realized I'd nothing for her. If there was one thing a proud mare didn't like, it was her expectations not being met. Apparently, she'd been undisturbed by the monster's presence earlier. I said a quick prayer of thanks that she'd been way up here at the time. Ríona stood next to me, rubbing Bó's side, as one of the few people — aside from me — whom Bó tolerated. Bríd stood out beyond in the field with her arms crossed.

"*Oya!* Let's go, girls," she grumbled. "I'm tired, and I'd like a nap before dinner." She'd left Finbar at home, as she always did when we went to the village, and she was sometimes the grumpier for it. It was easy enough for people to accept Faolan as a part of our family — if they could get past his likeness to a wolf — but Finbar drew gazes wherever he went. It wasn't many people had a pet crow nowadays.

I sometimes wondered if that was why Bríd had taken to him so. With her long, fine black hair and perfect skin, Bríd was stunning. Heads tended to turn wherever she went. But she also didn't look like anyone else in Ballyconneely. Boys used to tease her that her real family was in Clifden — the single immigrant family in the area who'd come from China. The farce of the Doyle triplets had been the story of our family for longer than any of us could remember, but anyone could see the three of us weren't biologically related. Ríona had the thick, dark curls of our mother's ancestors from Nigeria and the light brown skin that could have made her the biological daughter of our mother and father; I had the pale skin and fiery red hair that might've been Dad's Celtic genes; and Bríd was left with whispers from neighbors and the other kids in town. It didn't bother us, most of the time, because we were sisters, as truly as anyone could be.

"Come feckin' on, Moira!" Bríd called. "You can visit with your cow later."

"I will come see you later, girl," I whispered, rubbing Bó's nose.

"Jaysus, look at us," Bríd grumbled. "Normal girls would be planning a great big bash for their eighteenth."

"Normal girls?" I repeated, jumping off the wall and heading for the lane. Faolan ran ahead of us, yapping happily. "We are normal, Bríd."

Bríd scoffed. "Normal girls have a big do at the local pub with all their friends and the boys from the boys' school. They'd have a giant cake made by the bakery and probably their hair done all special. But not us." She kicked at a rock in the lane, sending dirt every which way. "What'll we do, girls? Sit by the fire and play feckin' whist?"

I didn't mention that we couldn't even do that — half the deck had gone into the fire in Bríd's anger at losing the last time we'd played cards together.

"Dad will be home by then," I said impatiently. But Ríona caught my gaze, and I felt a twinge in my gut. It was an empty promise, and she knew it. I had no more notion of Dad's return than either of them. And if the unease they felt was anything like mine, none of us were at all sure when that would be.

A great growl stopped us all short.

Faolan stood, up ahead, rigidly crouching before a startled hound. With one great bark, he lunged forward.

Gasping, Ríona sprinted toward the dueling dogs. "Faolan, no!" I shouted, as if the dog had ever heeded any words at all. No, the only commands he followed were the silent ones that passed between him and Ríona.

But he'd never attacked another animal before, either, so all bets were off.

The hound growled in defense and writhed away from Faolan, who was all legs and shaggy, red fur. Just then a body — a human body — stepped bravely between them. A boy no older than us spread his arms wide to protect the hound. Ríona reached them just in time to haul Faolan back by the scruff of the neck.

"God, I'm so sorry," I panted, reaching them as the boy turned to check his dog for injuries. Ríona held Faolan in a firm grip, staring into his amber eyes as his growl pathetically died in his throat. The two communicated on a level nobody else could understand.

"It's okay," the boy said, turning back to us and taking us in, as we did him. He was tall and lean, with pale, clear skin, dark auburn hair and bright gray eyes above sharp cheekbones. "Conry appears to be unhurt." His smile came easily.

Ríona tentatively released Faolan and when he made no move toward the hound, just giving a big huff of resentment, she let go and stood, looking shyly at the boy.

"The big eejit doesn't usually act like that," Bríd spoke up. And she was right. Faolan was a shy, aloof dog who had interest in no creature on Earth but Ríona. What had gotten into him? "But we'll make sure it doesn't happen again," Bríd promised him, smiling sweetly as she stepped forward. To my dismay, I saw both my sisters were quite taken. They each showed it in their own way. Ríona with her gaze darting from the stranger to the dirt beneath her feet, and Bríd with a smile fit to slay an army.

"No bother," the boy said, smiling back. He looked from Faolan up to Ríona, and her cheeks went red. "I'm going to take Conry home anyway. He seems a bit shaken. Though it's only his pride that's hurt. His name means 'king of the hounds,' you know. It may very well be revoked after that."

"Ah, but Faolan is no hound," Bríd said, laughing.

"I can see that." The boy's eyes seemed stuck on Faolan for a moment before he smiled and nodded politely, glancing at Rí one more time before turning to cut across the nearest field, his dog at his heels.

"Jaysus, girls." Bríd sighed. "We're just drowning in strange gorgeous boys today, aren't we?"

It was true. And I didn't like it.

an printíseach
THE APPRENTICE

ríona

The market was buzzing when we reached town, and it set my teeth on edge. The feel and the sound and the smell of so many bodies in one place made my mind race. All their thoughts were inching toward me, poking at me, interrupting my own. It wasn't something I usually had to worry about on the rustyback hill, but summers always meant a crowd in town. It wasn't that our corner of Connemara was interesting enough to draw so many tourists as the likes of Dublin or Galway, but we got our fair share, and anyway, summers were short in Ireland and every soul on this rock took every sunny opportunity handed to them.

Faolan's back slipped beneath my palm, and I let his soft fur calm me.

We both need to calm ourselves. He nudged my palm with his wet nose so I'd know he'd heard me.

I had no idea what had sparked his temper tantrum on the way to

town, but I'd held his head in my hands and felt the aggression drain from him and flow over my palms like water. Now, I felt only a nervous energy in him, an energy like that always pouring off Bríd. That was how I felt things. The things that didn't belong to me. They were an endless sea of thoughts and sensations outside myself that I couldn't control, only feel. It's not that I could read people's minds. Or know what they were thinking. It was more that I could *feel* it. See it, sometimes. It had always been that way. But most days I wished it wasn't.

Today, there were more stalls in the market than usual because a few of the local school children had set up their own stalls to showcase things they'd made and raise money for some charity or another. They were selling off drawings and trinkets, and I paused to look at a small ceramic dog. It was really quite well done.

"I heard she's mad."

It was the little girl behind the booth, her hand cupped around her mouth toward her friend. Amusement jumped off her, a sparkling halo. Faolan harrumphed, but I ignored them.

Of course I was used to the whispers, but that didn't mean I was impervious to them. They didn't even have to voice their feelings for me to know what they were thinking. When I was younger, I used to stay up late kneeling beside my bed, praying for the castle to materialize a hat that would obscure others' feelings — or maybe a cloak that would let me walk the market unseen.

Another little girl piped up. "She's just challenged, Sarah, don't be cruel." Her excitement over being in the market today was a golden halo around her, too, but hers was softer.

"I'm just saying what's true," the first snapped.

"Come, Rí," Bríd said loudly, glaring at the little girls as she linked her arm through mine. Her presence enveloped me in warmth. "We wouldn't waste our money on this feckin' rubbish." She shuffled me off to catch up with Moira, who was, as usual, all business and already halfway to Daniel Sheehan's stall.

Bríd's angry energy swirled around me in a dizzying tornado, but it was somehow comforting, like a knight brandishing a sword in your defense. She was like that. She'd be away wrapped up in herself or a new boy and the world as it related to her, until suddenly she was stepping in to bring you out of a dark corner and into her light, all when you didn't even think she'd noticed you. Faolan protectively lingered behind us, and Bríd didn't let go of my arm until we reached Daniel Sheehan's stall.

The old farmer lived just a few fields down from the rustyback, but we really only ever saw him at the market. It wasn't like we held dinner parties in the castle or went visiting neighbors. But his was the only stall in town that ever had yams or plantains, and his wife was the only other person in town who knew ISL. She'd taught it to me, when I was just tall enough to reach up around Mam's waist and cry in frustration. It had been Mam's idea, for me to learn ISL, and then all the rest of them, too, though her sudden death had stopped us from getting very much past the basics. Still, Mrs. Sheehan always had a kind sign and a smile for me. And Daniel Sheehan was kind to us, too. I'd never felt anything but friendliness from him, even when he was tired or frustrated or upset. Of course, my sisters didn't know that; they only knew he didn't gossip about us like the others did — or at least he did it when we weren't around. And I had a sneaking suspicion we were the only people in Ballyconneely who ever bought the plantains, but he got them special in from Dublin anyway.

"Why, look who it is," a deep, genial voice said as we studied the dusty veg on offer in the Sheehan stall. I registered Faolan's bristling fur beneath my fingers only a second before I looked up.

Bríd and I gaped at the same time, but Moira was already scowling at the boy behind the table.

It was the boy from the lane. The one whose dog Faolan had found issue with. *Relax*, I told Faolan silently.

Faolan snorted and stamped a paw. I tucked a coil of hair behind my ear.

The stranger put his hands up in the air. "Is it safe to speak to you?" he asked, his bright gray eyes on me. "Or should I worry about ending up like Conry?"

It had frightened me, the way Faolan had reacted — and the way he was reacting now — but a tiny piece of me found it thrilling, too. Because I seemed to be imagining that the boy looked at me a bit more than the boys in town usually did, and I let my mind wander so far as to wonder if that was why Faolan had his hackles up. Maybe it wasn't all in my head. Maybe he'd noticed it, too.

"I do believe you said your dog was fine," Bríd said, a smile twisting her lips.

"Oh, he is," the boy said, winking at her. "But I don't fancy a scare like he had today."

"Who are you, anyway?" Bríd asked brightly as Moira sighed none too quietly and turned her attention to turnips. I was too invested in the strange appearance of a boy who actually saw me to worry about what we were having for dinner.

Who is he?

Faolan snorted once more and sat back on his haunches. My interest was clearly annoying him.

"My name's Louis," the boy said, extending a hand to Bríd, and my eyes caught on the tattoo on his forearm. He extended his hand to me next. Moira had wandered down to the far end of the table, probably on purpose, so he only gave her a small salute. His skin was pale, and he didn't exactly look like the kind of boy used to working a farm, but his face was open and earnest, and the red strands of his auburn hair shone bright in the sun.

"So, Louis, what brings you to godforsaken Ballyconneely?" Bríd asked the question burning in my brain. "Because we've been here all our lives, and we've never seen you." Not to mention he had a slight English twinge to his words, and he dressed better than any boys we knew. No checked shirt or mud-caked wellies in sight.

"You know, I'm getting that a lot lately," Louis said, chuckling. "What is it about this town and being suspicious of strangers?"

"Suspicious?" Bríd repeated. "When you've been the odd ones out as long we have, the arrival of a new stranger for all the neighbors to gawk at is quite welcome, like."

Louis tilted his head. "And what exactly makes you all the odd ones out?" he asked. I was expecting the way he glanced at me then, but I wasn't expecting his gaze to linger, as if he wanted the answer from my own lips.

Do you have all day? I laughed. Faolan smacked me in the back of the knees with his snout. I ignored him.

For the first time today, instead of recoiling inside myself, I let my senses open. Reaching. Feeling. But as much as I tried, tried to feel something, an energy, a thought, a sense, from this boy, I couldn't. The older man beside us at the stall was worried, frazzled beyond measure, as he dug in his pockets for money, and the woman at the next stall over was a bright bundle of besotted light as she gazed on baker James Lynch and fumbled through his baked goods. But from Louis, I couldn't feel anything. Nothing at all.

I tried again, taking a deep breath and clearing my mind of everyone around me. Slowly, I tuned back into the world in front of me, inch by inch. It wasn't as easy as that. Everything came rushing back in, flooding my brain. But nothing, nothing from Louis.

"Well?" he said, glancing at Bríd.

"Let's just say we're different," she said, grinning mysteriously as she turned and walked down the length of the stall. "So tell me, stranger, how did you come to be manning Daniel Sheehan's stall, like? Don't tell me you've bought out the poor man. His family's been farming Ballyconneely for three feckin' generations."

Louis grinned. "Ah, I'm afraid to admit I don't have an acre to my name. That makes me pretty worthless around these parts, doesn't it?"

"That depends, like," Bríd simpered. "What else can you do?"

"Well, I think my current employer would say not much of anything," he quipped. "Mr. Sheehan's only letting me stay with him for the summer as a favor to my uncle. They're old friends from school, and Uncle Stephen needed to get me out of Derry for the summer."

"A fugitive, are you then?"

That from Moira. Bríd glared at her, her spirit souring around her, but I couldn't stifle a giggle. The thought of the gorgeous boy on the run from the guards in Northern Ireland was sort of exciting in a way. A fantasy that could entertain me for hours. My cheeks burned, and I fidgeted. Faolan was staring at me.

What? I turned slightly, so he couldn't see my face.

Despite her grouching, Louis smiled at Moira, all good nature and sparkling eyes. "Nothing quite so exciting as that, I'm afraid. Just an uncle who doesn't know what to do with me and thought a summer of work in the Gaeltacht would be good for my character or something."

"Ah, an Gaeilgeoir," Bríd said, brightening again.

Louis stared at her, a slow smile spreading across his face. "Was that Irish? The summer's only just begun. Give me a week at least to learn the basics." His accent didn't sound much like the Ulster accent, but the way his voice elongated the vowels was charming nonetheless.

"Grand," Bríd said. "I'll check in on you in a week. You'd best know the important bits by then, j'know? Like how to ask a girl out." She winked at him.

Louis glanced at me. "Well, like I said, there's not much of anything I'm very good at, so you might have to make it two weeks."

"Nonsense, Louis," Daniel Sheehan said, plopping an overflowing box of carrots on the table in front of the boy. His aura was a softly drifting thing that felt sometimes a little preoccupied, bumping absentmindedly into others', but always friendly. "There's plenty you're good at. You've already been a great help to me, and you haven't been here two days."

"You flatter me, Mr. Sheehan," Louis said, shaking his head at Bríd and me.

"What's that you've got there, Ríona?" Daniel Sheehan asked.

I realized I'd been nervously fidgeting with the coin from our little miraculous potted plant. Shrugging, I held it out.

Daniel Sheehan whistled. "That's a 1937 half crown, that is," he said with a surprised smile. "Are you collecting, Ríona?"

I glanced at Moira and then Bríd, who shrugged. Mr. Sheehan was looking at me, so I shook my head.

"Ye don't know, do you?" He smiled and held up the coin. "This, girls, is a pre-decimal half crown. It'd be worth hundreds of euro nowadays. See that sheen on it? If it's uncirculated, it could go for over a thousand euro."

My gaze snapped to Bríd's, then to Moira's. She stared back, her mouth open in surprise.

"We-We did know that," Bríd said quickly, plucking the coin out of Daniel Sheehan's hand. "Girls, are ye ready to head?" Flustered, she turned away from the stall, and I grinned as I went after her. It seemed the castle knew *exactly* what century it was. My sisters didn't always think the most of the castle's power, but I knew it had ways of knowing what we needed and when.

"What about your veg?" Sheehan called after us as we scurried away.

"Send it on with your new apprentice, would you?" Bríd called over her shoulder with a wink at Louis. "It's much too far for us to lug home!"

Moira groaned audibly and went back for our dinner, pausing to pick out a dozen eggs as well. After all, we'd soon be experiencing a small windfall. Bríd only smiled and dashed on toward home. She had always been a flirt. Probably since the day she'd jumped out of the womb ready to take on the world. But I took things slow and steady and watched the dramas of the world play on from the back row.

Even so, I couldn't help imagining that, as Louis waved good-bye, he was looking at *me*. As if to confirm my suspicions, Faolan gave a rough bark at the boy and turned haughtily toward home.

fara cailín

A GIRL'S ROOST

bríd

When I woke, my mattress lowered to my bed frame with a soft thump. I needed to stop sleeping on a feckin' curio. My old floral sheets were soaked with sweat, and my heart was clobbering my chest. I'd had the nightmare again. No matter what I did to calm my mind before sleep, I always drifted off with the fear in my gut. The fear that my mind would go there in my slumber. That I would see my sister die again.

Tonight was no different. My eyes stared into the dark, adjusting to it, and then searched the corner above me for the familiar sight.

Finny, tell me I'm fecking sane…

On a good night, the light of the moon would glint off Finbar's inky head. But tonight, the moon was hidden. Heavy clouds had rolled in just before sundown, and now all I could make out was the vague shape of his nest. It rested wedged atop the broken door to my room, which had been leaning against the wall these five plus years. Dad had

tried to take the door away to use as kindling one night, but I couldn't let him have Finbar's roost. At least some things were sacred. And one of those things was home. There was a soft coo from the corner.

I smiled. Sometimes Finbar's presence was the only thing keeping me from feeling completely fecking alone. People would say I was so lucky to have two sisters my age. Two friends to grow up with. And they were right. But that doesn't always stop the loneliness, j'know? There were some things I couldn't tell even my sisters. And it was nights when I hid those secrets that felt the darkest.

Down below me, I heard a door open and then close. It would be Moira, letting Bó in out of the storm. The mare would spend the night in the hall, where animals had been kept centuries before her. It had been a way of providing heating for the family, keeping animals on the first floor. Of course, I would hardly get any of that heat from Bó up here on the sixth floor.

That's how tall our tower house was, one room stacked on top of another, with me at the very top. I used to fancy myself a damsel in distress, being kept prisoner by her evil family. But that was the stuff of fairy tales. The truth was, once upon a time, this room would have been a great banquet hall where Irish chieftains entertained their clans or other visitors. There was a great, wide fireplace on the north wall, but it was a later addition. Originally, the fire would have been built right here in the middle of the room, where I lay every night, my heart beating double-time and my limbs fluttering with the will to move. I felt it, always, the wind flowing through my veins. Squeezing my eyes shut, I tried to imagine slow flames licking up the sides of my bed, a sad attempt to summon some warmth, some distraction, from fires of centuries past.

Shifting deeper under my covers, I felt something graze my fingers where I'd tucked them under my pillow. Pushing the pillow aside, I reached out and found … a trio of small stones. I smiled again. Gifts from Finbar. Or pranks. It was difficult to tell. There was nothing a crow loved more than mischief. But my crow also loved me. I would take his surprises either way.

Scooping the stones into my palm, I placed them on the short wooden table beside my bed. Tonight's discovery joined gifts past: a small, shiny ring missing its stone, a dried-up beetle, and the crumpled petal of a daisy.

Curling onto my side, I stared at Finbar's presents, these tiny signs of love, and willed my mind blank. Eventually, I fell asleep.

deirfiúracha sa stoirm
SISTERS IN THE STORM

bríd

I was awake before the thunder rumbled through the old walls, shaking everything in the castle. No, it wasn't the thunder that woke me. It was the screaming.

"God, Brí, wake up!" Moira's hands shook my shoulders, her palms clammy. "You're okay, Brí. Wake up!"

I was the one screaming.

Snapping my mouth shut, I gulped in air. The stale, peaty air of my room. My mattress stilled, falling back to the bed frame with a soft whisper of cloth on ancient wood.

Finbar sat on the headboard, which was long scratched and marked from his talons, his beak gently nudging my ear.

"I'm sorry," I breathed to no one in particular, my heart trying to beat out my chest.

"Sorry," Finbar squawked in his otherworldly way. "Sorry."

"Feck. I had a nightmare," I murmured.

"Clearly," Moira said with a sigh, pushing my hair out of my sweaty face. "What was it about?"

This wasn't the first time I'd woken Moira with my nightmares, but I'd never shared with her what I'd seen in the darkness. Tonight, it had been the same as any other, but this time, the mad horse from earlier had made an appearance. Its foaming mouth and rolling eyes came to me, real as anything, even now as I was awake.

Thunder cracked again, echoing around the tall, vaulted cathedral ceiling, and I startled.

"It's okay," Moira said, sliding under my old quilt and curling her arm around my shoulders. For all the annoyance she brought on us, Moira's gift for being motherly was sometimes just what I needed. Tonight, her arms felt as warm and secure as our mother's. Though sometimes I wasn't sure I was remembering her correctly. "It's okay."

Rain lashed against the castle, the old window panes rattling in a ghostly orchestra. Even the bats were tucked fearfully away in the bartizans off Ríona's room, as if they, too, knew that monstrous creature was still out there. Somewhere. Whether it was far or near, it turned my blood cold just to know it was alive.

At least I knew that wasn't how Moira would … well, I knew it wasn't a serious danger to her. If my dreams were to be believed.

"Come here, Rí," Moira said, and only then did I notice Ríona lingering by the door in her night gown, an old silk scarf of Mam's tied around her thick ringlets, frizzy from a day tramping about outside. "But watch your step."

Ríona dashed through the big room like she was running for cover, slipping and sliding on the books, clothes, and old curios strewn about my floor all around my big four-poster bed smack dab in the middle of the room. Dodging one of the buckets placed under a leak in the ceiling, she jumped onto the bed and climbed under the quilt as Moira and I squished together to make room for her. Faolan was at her heels, only, tonight, he didn't snuggle up at our feet like our own fur blanket, as the castle's inhabitants of old would have. He sat upright and alert at the foot of the bed, his gaze on the window.

"What were you dreaming, Bríd?" Moira asked me gently as she turned to braid Ríona's long hair.

I swallowed and felt the scratch of Finbar's feet on my arm. I looked into his eyes, and he cocked his head at me, as if he, too, wanted to know what went on in my head.

"Sorry?" Finbar repeated.

It hurt me to lie to him, or my sisters, but I had no choice. "I ... I saw Dad. He was in trouble, like. With ... with the guards." It wasn't a complete fabrication to say I worried about Dad getting into trouble with the police, but it wasn't what I'd dreamt. Far from it.

Moira sighed. "God, I'm worried, too," she admitted. "It's been far too long. I can't remember the last time he stayed away so long."

Ríona squeezed my hand painfully, and I knew she was doing the same to Moira. Ríona wasn't able to voice the words in her head, but she had other ways, and they always managed to say what no one else would. But tonight, her having to reassure us only served to highlight that we'd been contemplating the alternative. That Dad was absolutely not okay.

Another flash of lightning lit the room in a garish mockery of daytime.

"Looks like he was right," Moira said thoughtfully. She squeezed her eyes shut as another bout of thunder rocked the bed.

"Who?" I asked, breathing deeply, trying to dull the constant movement in my veins.

"The boy who saved your life."

Yes, he had said it would storm. How had he known that? Where had he come from?

And, more importantly, how had he singlehandedly fought off a monster to save my life?

an t-ionróir

THE INVADER

moira

"No! God! The washing!" I cried, dashing toward the door.

"It's been raining all night, Moira!" Bríd called after me, poking at her eggs as her foot tapped the floor. She hadn't eaten much of anything all morning, and I blamed the nightmares. But whatever went on in her slumbering mind she wouldn't share with me. "D'you really think you're going to salvage the washing now? It's all soaked, to be sure."

Of course she was right, but I didn't thank her for sharing such opinions when she never lifted a finger to help. Rolling my eyes, I wrenched open the heavy door that led to the kitchen garden, a tiny walled area that Dad had rigged up with washing line going every which way. Four people could sure make a lot of laundry, and sometimes it was a wonder our damp clothing didn't bring the crumbling ancient walls down completely.

"Let's focus on something important!" Bríd called from the kitchen. "Like what eejit we're going to sell that farthing to!"

"It's a half crown!" I shouted, shutting the door behind me.

A good portion of the laundry was on the ground and I stifled an annoyed groan. Not only would it have to be dried again — it would have to be washed again. Sighing, I reached for the nearest shirt of Dad's that had stayed put on the line; might as well salvage what I could. As it flapped in the breeze, I caught sight of movement near the back of the garden.

"Hello?" I called. There was a small arched opening in the wall that let out to the corner of the bailey Bó liked best. But the doorway was too small and the grass too sparse to tempt Bó or any wandering animals.

Suddenly, I thought of the murderous horse that had nearly killed my sister. *That* creature had been scared of nothing.

"Shoo!" I called out in a strangled voice, my heart pounding.

There was a flash of blue between the pillowcases I'd carefully hung on the line yesterday. A flash of something large and upright. Something that wasn't an animal.

"Is someone there?"

If it was Brian Brennan or one of the lads from the village having a laugh, I'd give him an earful. The only way to catch him in the act was to cut off his access to the arch—

My eyes fell on him as I stepped in front of the opening. He wasn't trying to escape. He was crouching in the dirt, his weight resting against the wall. And he was shirtless.

No, not Brian Brennan.

"You're—

"S-Sorry," the boy from the sea said in a stutter, clutching a blue checked shirt against his midsection. A familiar shirt. A shirt I'd hung on the line myself …

"Are you stealing my father's clothes?" I asked incredulously.

"I'm sorry — I was just —"

"God, you're bleeding!" I gasped.

He'd moved Dad's blue shirt from in front of him in supplication, revealing a gash of red across his middle.

"What-What happened?" I asked, wringing my hands. "And why are you in our garden?"

"You … You live here?" he asked, looking over his shoulder at the disintegrating edifice of Bunrowan Castle. His hair was wet and messy across his forehead, and *he* was the one trespassing in *my* garden, but still, my cheeks burned a little. I knew it didn't look like much, the old castle, from the outside. Or the inside, for that matter. But it was home.

"Yes," I said firmly. "And you're trespassing. And … you really need to see a doctor."

"No!" he said quickly.

That was an absurd reaction to such a sensible suggestion. Was this boy wanted by someone? Like the police?

"Then maybe the guards," I said, folding my arms over my chest. "For trespassing *and* attempted theft."

"No, please. I just … I lost my clothes, and I saw these … "

"You *lost* your *clothes*?" I repeated.

He nodded, his eyes pleading. He really had the most peculiar way of looking at you. Like you were a creature he'd never seen before … and was mildly afraid of. And that, I suppose, is what made me wonder.

"It's Aidan, isn't it?" I asked. He nodded, clutching the shirt to his stomach again. I couldn't tell if he was cold or trying to staunch the bleeding, but either way, I didn't think Dad would be getting that shirt back. "Aidan, where's your home? Do you have a place to go?"

"Uh, that's a complicated question, actually," he murmured.

"Moira! Ríona's being feckin' thick about giving up that damn coin, and the plant is taking *so* long to grow—"

The nearest hanging pillowcase was ripped aside, and Bríd froze, the potted plant in her hands. Her knuckles went white around it as she took in the scene in the garden. Finbar landed on her shoulder, his head cocked.

"Damn coin," he mimicked, like a toddler learning to speak. "Damn coin."

Aidan's eyes flashed to the bird in alarm. Few people would be comfortable with Finbar's ghostly attempts at human speech, and that was yet another reason we kept him from the village.

"Moira?" Bríd said, her voice strangled, and I knew what she was thinking. Only one of us had ever been caught in the garden with a shirtless boy, and it wasn't worth pretending the whole world couldn't guess which sister that had been.

"Don't look at me," I said quickly. "I don't know what's going on. He scared me half to death. But he's bleeding all over the roses like a stuck pig. And I don't think he has a place to go."

Aidan looked at the ground, his brow furrowed. Of course there were no roses, just weedy, scattered grass, but there would have been at one time in a garden like this.

"No-No," he said in a stutter, frowning at me, "you've misunderstood." He climbed to his feet with one hand braced against the wall, the other pressing Dad's shirt to his wound. "I'm just trying to get home. I'm really, really far from home."

"America," Bríd said.

"America," Finbar said.

It wasn't a question. There was no mistaking the clear, even American accent. Even out here, we heard it often enough. There was no escaping Americans in this country. Or on the telly.

"Where did you sleep last night?" Bríd asked, her nose wrinkled. "Were you staying with someone in the village?"

I could tell we were having the same thought: it looked as though he'd slept on the beach.

"No, I—" Aidan must have realized his mistake because he snapped his mouth shut and paused. "I just need a little help."

"Like directions to a doctor?" Bríd asked.

"No," he said firmly.

"America," Finbar squawked.

"Just, just some water to clean up with," Aidan said, tearing his eyes from the shiny black bird on Bríd's shoulder. The pair of them were a sight, I knew that. Bríd, with her striking black hair and pink lips, the sleek, loyal bird following her every move. Of course it wouldn't escape Aidan's notice. "A-And a clean shirt," he added. "And maybe ... if you have any money to spare." His gaze darted to the ground.

The ground here was mostly dirt, with weak sprouts of grass poking through where the sun shone every now and again. The longer he was out here, the dirtier he'd get, and with that wound...

Bríd *tsked*. "We've got water aplenty," she said, gesturing toward the sea, "but I'm afraid money doesn't grow on trees around here." Her fingers tightened around the potted plant and she twittered at her own joke, twirling back toward the castle. "Let me consult my sisters for a moment," she said to Aidan. "Moira, come!"

Ríona had her face pressed against the splinter in the small window of the kitchen. There was the tiniest hole at the intersection of the cracks, and I knew from experience that if you pressed your ear against it, you could hear what your sister was saying to a boy hiding in the garden. I'd just never been the object of such spying before.

"We have to let him in," Bríd pronounced before I'd even closed the door behind me. Faolan stood just inside the door, trying to peek out.

"But then he'll know we're alone," I said, biting my lip. As much as I wanted to help him, especially after what he'd done for Bríd, every warning Dad had ever imparted upon us before the thousands of trips he'd taken in our lifetime came ringing back through my ears.

"It's the safest place in Ireland," he always said with a smile, because everyone knew neither of the two doors to the castle had working locks. Then his face would sober up and he'd say, "All you have to do is keep to the castle, and the castle will take care of you." When we'd been tiny, before bed, Mam would tell us the story of why she'd planted the Whitethorn and Blackthorn on either side of the path at the front door. The faerie tree for company, she'd say of the Whitethorn, for they are the assembly places of the otherworld. And the Crone of the Woods, the tree of ill omen, the Blackthorn, for protection. "For where the Blackthorn grows near her sister, the Whitethorn, the hawthorn, the land is especially magical." I could hear her voice, even now, certain syllables reflecting the accent of her parents, as deep and gentle and warming as ever. Death hadn't chilled that part of her. And it wouldn't remove her stories.

"Keep to the castle," Dad would add knowingly as Mam had kissed us each on the forehead before bed, "and the castle will take care of you."

He always said it. Always. But it wasn't exactly an admonishment to keep others *out* of the castle, was it?

"He's bleeding, Rí," Bríd said, hugging the potted plant to her chest. She was trying to get Ríona to team up against me. And it worked. Ríona smiled indulgently at me and pretended to punch my arm.

We have you, she signed.

"She's right, like," Bríd said, precariously gesturing with the pot. "We all know you can hold your own against a boyo like that. Especially when he's injured."

It wouldn't be the first time I'd come to blows with a boy. In fact, as a child, I'd had kind of a reputation for it. It used to drive our mother mad. Any time a boy had made Ríona cry, I'd launch into them, fists flying. Of course, it hadn't taken much to scare them off. I'd already had a reputation. I'd been faster than any of them, and I'd beaten half the lads in the village in some race or game or another. They hadn't exactly taken kindly to that, at any age, and I hadn't been allowed to play football with them after a time.

"You're inhumanly fast," a boy named Colin had said to me once.

"Have you met her sisters?" Brian Brennan had piped up. "They're all inhuman."

And the looks on their faces had told me it hadn't been a compliment. That might've been the point I'd stopped trying to fit in and retreated into our own little world on the rustyback hill. Once Dad had started homeschooling us — or, rather, Ríona, the resident book nerd, had started leading us in our lessons — it had been easy to retreat for good.

So it had been a long time since I'd had to defend myself or one of my sisters. But I'd *almost* had to — yesterday. For the first time in a very long time. But I hadn't in the end. Because this very boy had saved us.

"Arah, fine," I said quietly, "but we have to be careful. Don't tell him anything about us. Or the castle."

Bríd dashed to the door, dirt tumbling out of the pot clutched to her stomach, and nudged Faolan out of the way. The big dog followed her outside and cocked his head at the stranger. His hackles were down, and that comforted me for reasons I couldn't put into words.

Aidan was still standing braced against the garden wall, one hand clutched around his middle.

"Well, the council has conferred," Bríd said brightly, "and decided that you are most welcome to Bunrowan Castle." She flourished one arm in front of her like a grand old dame.

A weary sigh escaped the strange boy, and he forced a smile onto his lips. "Thank you," he said, his eyes on me.

déan dearmad air
FORGET ABOUT IT

ríona

"I'm afraid you have to wait for the water heater to get going and then fill the tub," Moira explained, "as it won't stay warm long enough for a proper shower."

Bathrooms in the castle were an awkward affair, shoehorned into a structure not meant to hold them. There were three, and Bríd had wanted to show our visitor to the best one, but that was the one in my room. The fourth floor of the tower house was mine, and every inch of the expansive room was stuffed full of curios that hadn't interested Dad's clients — and of course also a sleeping wolf. To have the boy pick through that obstacle course on his way to the bath would be a dangerous game, indeed.

Instead, Moira had sighed and led him to her own domain on the fifth floor. It had a tub the size of a small dog, but it would be far safer — as long as he didn't notice the trap door in the ceiling.

I hung back near the stairs, absentmindedly clutching the rough rope that wound along the staircase in the corner of the castle. It was a counterclockwise spiral of uneven steps meant to trip up invaders and impede their swords. I stared at the strange boy as Moira showed him how to turn off the immersion. Trippy stairs or no, he'd still managed to get in. And his energy was more mutinous than Bríd's. It had alarmed me at first, down by the beach, but I figured that was the only way he'd been able to take on that creature. They shared that animalistic energy. But now, here he stood in front of me, calm as anything, while energy crashed off him and around him and into him in waves. Almost like he couldn't control it, like it existed outside himself. And every so often, all of it would cease, quite suddenly, and fall to the ground like a breaking wave. All would be calm, a match to his tranquil exterior. I'd never seen anything like it before. And it made me wonder: were there two sides to this boy? I'd never met a person with such contrasting feelings. I didn't know what it meant. But I did know he seemed to need help from a Good Samaritan or three.

I only hoped we didn't come to regret it.

Either way, Dad would be livid when he heard about this. But Bríd was right. It was the only kind thing to do. The boy, Aidan, was injured. Besides, Faolan was slumbering peacefully downstairs in his den of old blankets. I could feel his serene snores from here, which meant we couldn't be in any real danger. He'd never failed me before.

Moira shooed me downstairs to the drawing room, where Faolan met us, dragging his blanket along, and Bríd waited with her arms crossed and a smirk on her face. "I've never been so disappointed not to have a bath in my room," she said conspiratorially. "After all, he is *my* knight in shining armor, technically speaking."

Moira rolled her eyes. "It's quite lucky for him you don't, actually."

Bríd smirked. "But I do have a trap door."

I couldn't suppress a giggle, but Moira was unamused. "God, you can truly think of nothing else, can you?" she said darkly. "Is it the attention you crave? Do you get some sort of thrill from always making a scene of yourself?"

Bríd's mood soured, and I knew Moira was being too harsh. Bríd didn't like the attention, not one whit, but she would get it whether she wanted it or not, and this was how she coped. By throwing it right back in others' faces.

"If you don't keep your mind on the things in this world that actually matter," Moira went on, truly on a matronly rant now, "you're going to end up in prison for who-knows-what, and you can bet I won't be coming to bail you out!"

Bríd rolled her eyes and went to stand against the wall, pulling one leg up to rest against her thigh and closing one eye. I could feel her breaths lengthening and slowing. Faolan was already curled up in his favorite dingy blue blanket by the fire, as useless as a brick during most daylight hours. The minute the mysterious blanket had appeared at the foot of my bed, Faolan had made it his own. When you wrapped yourself up in it, the soft cotton silenced the noises of the world around you. Literally. There was little a hibernating pup wanted more. I just wished it would work on people's thoughts and feelings and not just the noises they made.

"Come, Rí, let me do your hair," Moira said with a sigh.

I sat on the floor in front of the couch, and Moira set to work braiding my hair for bed. She was about as useless with beauty routines as I was, but when our mother died, Moira had naturally taken over our nightly rituals. And Mam had always braided my hair in thick, hanging braids before bed so my curls would be full and well-defined the next day, or wrapped it one of her silken scarves to keep the frizz away. I wasn't one for strict beauty regimens, but these were things I would always do. My hair was the one thing of my mother's I carried with me every day. Faolan curled up beside me, and I buried my fingers in his fur as I thought about what had brought the strange boy from the sea to us — and a little about Daniel Sheehan's new apprentice, too. With Faolan beside me, I felt no fear. But I had reason enough to admit it was strange, our meeting two new boys in as many hours.

What does it mean?

Faolan only sighed in his sleep.

Moira tied off the last braid with a piece of cloth and released me. "Where will we put him?" she murmured some time later, more to herself than anyone else.

Bríd opened her other eye. "He's not a pair of feckin' socks, Moira, you don't 'put' him anywhere."

"But where will he sleep?"

I pointed at the stone floor. Dad's empty room was directly below us.

Moira bit her lip. Dad would hate the thought of a stranger in his room, that was for sure, but I also knew the fleeting look on Moira's face had nothing to do with that. She was tough and stern and dependable, but she embarrassed easily, though she tried to hide it. Dad's room was sparse and cold, the bed lumpy and sagging. He always saved every convenience for us, and his mind worked so rapidly, he was hardly present in the castle even when he was here. It was a game I liked to play. Sit near him and watch him sitting there right in front of me, even as his thoughts wandered far, far away. I could feel them growing softer and softer as they got farther and farther away. He certainly didn't notice a lumpy bed.

But this boy, Aidan, would. And he'd probably find Dad's old books and the disused chapel in the corner incredibly strange as well. Maybe a little creepy. And Moira didn't want that. I just wasn't sure why. He'd be gone and off away forever soon enough. Why did she care what he thought of us?

"No," she said carefully. "I think we should set him up in here. Dad wouldn't thank us for putting a stranger in his room."

"He's not going to thank us anyway," Bríd said, stifling a yawn. Her thoughts were as tangled and confused as ever, but moving a bit slowly, like they did only when she was exhausted. After all, today had been no ordinary day. "Jaysus, I'm wrecked. What is he doing up there? The water'll be cold by now."

A resounding shout filled the castle, followed by fierce splashing, a few thuds, and indignant squawking.

My eyes snapped to the ceiling, and all was frozen for a moment, not a movement in the atmosphere, before Bríd dashed for the door. Moira, Faolan, and I were on her heels, visions of sea monsters flying through our heads. It was a little odd, wasn't it, that the boy had "saved" us so quickly after that devil horse's arrival? What if he'd been the one to let the thing loose in the first place?

How could we be so stupid? Faolan barked sharply.

Judging by my sisters' speed, their thoughts were similar. We flew deftly up the stairs, snatching at the rope, skipping the stumbling steps and flying right past my room. Moira was ten steps ahead as usual when we reached her room, and she skidded to a halt in the doorway to the bathroom.

Aidan stood dripping in the middle of the tiny room, a towel wrapped around his waist and a sheepish look on his face. The soft sound of splashing drew our gaze to the tub — where Finbar splashed and preened gaily in the bathwater.

Bríd clapped a hand to her mouth to smother a laugh, and a smile broke out on my face, too. Faolan groaned.

"He scared me," Aidan admitted, running a hand through his hair, his eyes on the floor. His energy was at one of its uncharacteristic calm points, and I felt myself relax. Then my eyes lit on his midsection. An angry red gash ran across his middle, glistening red. We were all wedged in the doorway, and I glanced at Moira and Bríd, who gulped and plastered a smile onto her face. He'd sustained that horrible injury in her defense, and as the air quivered around her, I realized she felt embarrassed for it. But she would never say so.

"Jaysus, if that scared ya, it's a good thing we didn't use the trap door," she said with a wink.

"The what?" Aidan said, his eyes widening.

She pointed at the ceiling.

Aidan looked up and blanched. "Where does that go?" he asked, and his calm energy flipped into a frenzy at once. Still, he kept his composure on the outside. Like there were two persons inside him — this calm, composed boy, and another wild, more feral one — but he'd only let us see the one. How did he do that? In my experience, no matter how hard a person tried to hide their thoughts and feelings, they slipped through in tiny movements, small gestures. But Aidan ... Aidan held the mask firm.

"That goes to my room," Bríd said brightly. "This room used to be an *oubliette*, j'know? A tiny prison."

"Yes, but it's a toilet now," Moira said, walking up to the bath, carefully avoiding eye contact with the boy in a towel. "So we can go ahead and get that trap door sealed." She flicked water at Finbar, who screeched something that sounded mysteriously like a curse word in an American accent.

I wonder where he picked that up. I smothered a small smile.

"It's okay, Finny," Bríd cooed at him as he landed on her shoulder. "This is your house. That boy had no right to interrupt your bath."

Aidan was still staring up at the ceiling as Moira glared at Bríd and stepped out of the tiny room. "I'll get you something to clean that up with," she said with a vague nod at Aidan's middle and then she disappeared.

"This door was added later," Bríd said, tapping the bathroom door. "Originally, the only way in or out of the *oubliette* was through that." She pointed at the trap door. Her eyes never left Aidan, who gulped and glanced at her. "They'd throw their prisoners in and ... Do you know what *oubliette* means?"

Aidan shook his head.

"Forget about it."

He looked at her quizzically. "What does it mean?"

"That's what it means. Throw them in and *forget about it.*" Bríd's smirk was downright malevolent. There was little she enjoyed more than teasing boys.

"Do you ... ?" Aidan cleared his throat. "Do you scare all your visitors like this?"

Bríd laughed, and Finbar mimicked her in a barbaric imitation. "Silly lad, you're the only visitor we've ever had."

buíocḣas
GRATITUDE

a i d a n

There was a good chance I was going to die here. But I wouldn't fare much better outside. I just needed to decide whether I wanted to die by kelpie or teenage girl. It wasn't clear yet which would be less painful. And I was in enough pain as it was. I clutched my stomach.

"Here we are now." The one called Moira was back with a stack of clean white towels and a bottle of something brown. I straightened, letting my arms fall to my sides and clenching my teeth through the pain. Her eyes were on the slash on my abdomen, but she quickly averted them as she held the towels out to me.

"Thanks," I mumbled, hoping she'd leave now. I knew I was going to yelp or cry — or both — when I had to touch the cut, and it would be better for both of us if she didn't stick around to see that.

"Do you need help?" she asked, her eyes flicking to it again.

"It's nothing," I said. Nothing but some missing flesh torn out by a

kelpie.

"Okay." She hesitated a moment, then left the bathroom, softly closing the door behind her.

My entire stomach pulsed, and only a glance told me it needed some serious looking after. Bathing had done away with most of the blood, but the gash was deep. I changed into the pair of pants the girls had brought me earlier and then doused one of the clean towels in the murky-looking antiseptic. Sucking in a deep breath, I pressed it to the laceration.

The noise that erupted from my throat couldn't be called human.

Moira was back in an instant. She peeked in, clearly startled, but then realized she hadn't knocked and backed away again.

"It's okay. You can come in," I said. "I'm done. Do you think I should wrap it up?"

Stepping inside, she gave me the most maternal look I'd seen since … well, since Oyster Beach. "Arah, you can't have cleaned it properly now," she chided, taking the towel from me without further ado. "Here." She took the antiseptic, doused the towel again, and pressed it firmly against the wound.

I sucked in a breath through my teeth.

"Aidan," she said.

"Mm?" I couldn't form any words, because my lips were pressed firmly together to stop any more embarrassing sounds from escaping.

"Did you just happen to get in a particularly nasty fight down at the pub recently, or is this from … you know?"

I didn't want to make her feel responsible, so I didn't say anything. Finally, she took the towel away to be replaced with a clean one and glanced at me.

"Please tell me."

I sighed. "The k— ... I mean ... That horse. It did get a good bite in before I could scare it off."

Moira closed her eyes for a moment. Then she went back to fixing me up with another towel. I kept my teeth clenched, and by the time she was patting it dry, I almost felt numb. She had a large piece of cloth — it looked like a bedsheet — which she ripped into long strips now and wrapped around my middle. Her fingers were cold, but the chill was welcome because my skin felt like it was on fire. When she'd finally knotted the last strip, binding me up like a mummy, she stepped back and looked at the floor.

"I ... I wanted to say thank you," she said, her brow furrowed, like she wasn't sure how exactly to do this. "For ... For ... god, for saving my sister."

"You don't have to thank me," I said quickly.

"No, I do. I'm just not very good at it."

That made me smile a bit. "Not used to people helping you?"

"Not used to people," she murmured.

I smiled again. "Oddly enough, it's been a long time since I had to deal with people, too."

glaoch an dúchais
CALL OF THE WILD

moira

"I'm afraid it's the best we can do," I said, gesturing at the ring of dilapidated couches around the fireplace in the sitting room. I fiddled with a loose thread on the nearest mustard-yellow sofa.

"It's just fine, really," Aidan said quickly. But his eyes weren't on the mismatched couches in front of us. I watched him take in the vaulted ceiling and the tall mullioned windows, the biggest in the house but for those in Bríd's room. Beneath the tips of my fingers, I could still feel Aidan's skin, but I wouldn't be able to formulate words if I dwelled on that. It was entirely too hot in here. The flames in the fireplace were dying down, but Ríona was already rushing toward the stack of logs piled haphazardly against the wall. The stone behind the firewood was dirty and marked from years of stacks just such as this one. I'd never really noticed before. Clearing my throat, I tore my eyes from Aidan. What embarrassing accommodations we had to offer.

Like every other floor of the tower, the third floor was one large room. In the very beginning it would have been much like this, all bare stone fit for an Irish clan. In later days, it had been decorated by British nobles with giant paintings, sweeping curtains, sparkling chandeliers, and magnificent tapestries. Of course, all that had been sold by now. All that was left was the faint pale spots where the paintings and tapestries used to hang. It was a return to its origins. I liked it better this way.

But is that how Aidan saw it?

Of course the castle had certainly seen better days — probably feasts and battles alike. But most of it was just space now. Our family hosted neither feasts nor battles, and an old tower house has crannies and cracks enough to let in a full-scale gale. That meant most nights it was too cold to move very far from the fire. Even now, at the height of summer, most of the room was bare and uninviting, with all three couches scooted into a tight ring around the fire.

And in the middle of it was Faolan, who raised his head and yawned, his great skull limned in orange from the flames behind him. That's what Aidan was looking at now.

"He doesn't bite," Bríd said, which wasn't exactly true. There was plenty Faolan bit. He just hadn't made a habit of including humans in that category. Yet.

Swallowing nervously, Aidan walked around a bucket collecting rainwater from the ceiling and squeezed through two couches to gingerly sit on the faded red corduroy one Dad had brought back from one of his trips.

Ríona appeared with a limp pillow in her arms, which she proffered to Aidan. He took it from her gently, his movements slow, probably from the pain. Ríona gave him a friendly smile and backed away, but Faolan was at her heels, nudging the backs of her knees. The sun was settling behind the trees outside, so Faolan would want to be out now. The lazy thing was a rock for most of the day and night, but come dusk and dawn, he was more alive than any other dog I'd known, as active as the bats in the bartizans of the fourth floor.

I saw hesitation in Ríona's eyes and understood it immediately. She'd kept Faolan inside all night last night — he was no match for a sea monster — and the poor animal wasn't used to that at all. The only other time he'd been cooped up like that against his will was when he'd been just a pup and there'd been rumors of a rabid dog on the loose.

Faolan pawed the back of Ríona's leg and gave a low whine.

Aidan jumped back, sliding down the couch away from them.

Bríd stifled a laugh and plopped down on the other end of the corduroy couch. "I told you he doesn't bite," she chastised. Finbar hopped down from her shoulder, along her arm, and to the couch cushion beside her, cocking his head at the stranger.

"Does *he*?" Aidan muttered, glaring at Finbar.

"Ah, if he did, you'd have lost a finger long ago, j'know?" Bríd twittered.

"What is he?" Aidan asked, his eyes jumping back to Faolan. "The wolf thing."

"Do ye not have dogs in America?" Bríd asked, highly amused.

"That doesn't look like a dog," Aidan said, sitting up straighter, as if to fortify himself against these unimaginable circumstances he'd landed himself in. "It looks like a wolf."

"There are no wolves in Ireland," Bríd said, as if Aidan were a bit slow.

"Dad says he might be part wolf, somehow," I explained. "If someone had an illegal wolf somewhere. But it doesn't matter; he's gentle enough."

Just then, Faolan sat back on his haunches and gave an earsplitting howl at the ceiling.

Aidan jumped, his eyes wide as saucers, and immediately grimaced, clutching his stomach.

I bit my lip. Bríd stood and turned away from Aidan, putting a hand on Ríona's arm. "You have to let him out, Rí," she said gently. "He won't rest till you do, j'know?"

Ríona sighed. *I know*, she signed and extended her hand toward Faolan. He obediently placed his furry head in her palm, and she gave it two quick sweeps with her fingers, communicating on some level unknown to us, before heading for the door, Faolan running ahead of her.

"Where are they going?" Aidan asked, his eyes darting around the room, like we were about to lock him up to fashion some sort of boy vs. dog gladiator scenario for our own entertainment.

"He usually goes where he pleases, like, but she's had him locked up since yesterday," Bríd explained, falling back onto the couch with a huff. "And that's partly your feckin' fault."

"My fault?" Aidan repeated, his dark brown eyes wide. I had to look away quickly.

"Tell me you had nothing to do with that monster we saw yesterday," Bríd said, crossing her arms over her chest. Her face glowed in the fire.

"Tell me," Finbar squawked.

"How did you know how to fight it?" Bríd said. "You knew just what to do."

"I didn't!" Aidan snapped, leaning forward over his knees. "I—"

"Where did you come from?" Bríd demanded. "Why were you there at that exact moment? Why were you so close to our house?"

The questions came tumbling one after the other, giving Aidan no time to answer, not even leaving Finbar time to chime in. And for once, I didn't stop her, didn't tell her to lay off, to stop being so pushy. Because these were questions we should have asked before we'd let a stranger into our home.

"Answer me," Bríd said simply.

She didn't have to yell. Because boys always did what she wanted.

"I'm just trying to get home," Aidan said, staring at his splayed hands as if a monologue were written there. "It was a complete coincidence that I saw you in trouble with that k—" He gulped. "That horse."

"It wasn't a horse," Bríd whispered. Aidan looked at her, shadows dancing across his face. "It was a feckin' monster." She held his gaze, and he didn't break it for a long moment.

Finally, he said, "I just want to get home."

Bríd was silent as she turned her gaze to the fireplace. An old coat of arms was etched into the stone there, but it had long faded past recognition. There was no telling what clan it had once identified, the castle had changed hands as often as Ireland herself.

"Is home America?" Bríd asked quietly. I could see the ice melting away. He'd somehow convinced her he was just another boy. A boy who needed our help and one she apparently thought worthy of it.

"St. Louis," Aidan said quietly, nodding, not looking at either of us. "But I don't have any money."

Bríd was silent for a long moment. "We might have —"

"We don't," I interrupted, staring at her, hard. I knew what she was about to say. But we weren't going to let him know about the curios. That was out of the question.

"Look, I have family here," Aidan said desperately. "In Ireland. I … I think."

"You think?" I repeated.

"I … I'm not sure they're still here. But if they are, I can find them. They'll help me. I just need to find them."

I rolled my eyes. "Another American on some ridiculous ancestry journey? How exactly will that help you, pray tell?"

"No," Aidan said, shaking his head. His dark hair was just a bit damp from his bath, and it kept falling into his eyes. "I promise it's not like that. It's my brother. He lives here … or he did, last I saw him.

"How long has it been since you've seen him?" Bríd asked. "Is he likely to shove you out on your arse if we do find him?"

We? Had she really committed to this so easily?

I shifted my weight from one foot to the other, feeling this situation slip out of my hands completely.

Ríona still hadn't returned, and I was sure she was standing in the open door to the castle, nervously watching what little of the rustyback hill she could see in the light of the moon. But I had more faith in Faolan's ability to take on a sea monster than Ríona's.

"Brí, let's go check on Ríona," I said loudly.

Bríd looked at me, and there was no defiance in her eyes, like I'd expected. She was just as thrown off by this boy's story as I was. Nodding, she followed me down the stairs and around the storage room to the tiny entrance hall, where Ríona stood in the open door watching the bats flit across the light of the moon.

She gave us a weak smile and shivered, but Bríd was all business. "There's something he's not telling us," she pronounced, crossing her arms.

I sighed and rubbed my arms against the cold. "I know."

áit do ceann a leagadh
A PLACE TO LAY YOUR HEAD

a i d a n

The screaming woke me.

I'd been awake three or four times tonight before that, but this time I jumped right off the couch. It was coming from somewhere above me.

Could the kelpie have come back? Or something else? It wasn't the only strange creature around here.

Without thinking too much about the risks of running around a creepy medieval castle at night, I ran for the door to the stairwell, which was a spiral with uneven steps. It was ungodly dark, and I kept tripping, but the wailing didn't stop, so neither did I. My stomach ached from the movement, but I only pressed an arm to it and ran on.

The door to the fourth floor was flung open, but all was dark inside. The scream was coming from higher up. I kept going.

The door to the fifth floor was closed, and I heard scratching on

the other side of the door. I paused to listen. It was probably the wolf. The screaming was coming from higher still, so I thought of letting the beast out for a second line of defense against whatever I found on the next floor. But then again there was no telling whether the wolf-dog would just attack me instead.

Shaking my head, I dashed on up the stairs. And came to a dead end.

The sixth floor was the top floor. Turning to the open doorway to the sixth floor, I peeked inside. The door was off its hinges, leaning against the wall.

Moonlight was filtering through ornate windowpanes, revealing a huge room with a big bed right in the center. The loud sister with the dark hair was splayed across it, her head thrashing back and forth on her pillow as she screamed.

Relief flooded me. She was asleep. Just having a bad dream.

How stupid could I have been to think a kelpie had somehow made it to the top floor of an old castle to attack a girl? My brain was still foggy; I'd only been using it two days.

She moaned, and I hesitated at the door. *Should I leave her be?*

It was then that I noticed her mattress wasn't on the bed frame. It hovered a few inches above it. It was *levitating*.

My heart beat fast. Glancing quickly around to see if I'd be divebombed by her bird, I stepped into the room. And promptly tripped on something that clattered loudly.

The girl's screams died in her throat, and I paused, wondering if I should just leave her in peace — and maybe run for my life.

The floor was covered with stuff. A veritable field of landmines to walk across in the dark.

"No!" she shouted, bolting upright before screaming her head off again.

"Hey," I called, realizing how scary it would be to wake up to a guy creeping across your dark room in the middle of the night. "It's just me — Aidan!"

But she whimpered and moaned, and as she lay back down on the mattress, I realized she was still asleep. *Levitating*, but asleep. This was my imagination playing tricks on me. Right? Surely my stiff, out-of-practice brain was failing me.

"No!" she shouted again. "Please!"

I nudged aside whatever was at my feet, carefully picked my way to her bed, and shook her wrist. "Wake up! You need to wake up!"

ar sciathán préacháin
ON CROW'S WINGS

bríd

The wind rushed through my wings, and I couldn't land, much as I wanted to. Her body lay gently across the pebbles on the shore, but I wasn't in control. I couldn't reach it. And he stood there, at the water's edge, smoothing something in his hands.

Why won't you help her? I wanted to scream. But I couldn't. All that came out was a shrill, "Why? Why?"

Aidan took one step back toward the sea, and then the world shook. Everything shook.

The rocks below me. The waves in front of me. The clouds above me.

The pillow. The pillow beneath me.

I was in my room. My mattress thumped down against the bed frame.

Blinking, I looked at the shadowed ceiling high above me. It felt a

million miles away, my feet, my arms, my heart weighted to the earth. When all my body wanted to do was soar.

"Sorry," a figure in the dark said.

I stared hard and realized I was looking at a boy standing sheepishly beside my bed.

There was a sleepy squawk, and Finbar swooped drunkenly down to my headboard. He blinked at me, still half-asleep.

"Sorry," Aidan repeated, backing away from my bed. "You were screaming. And … And … " He tripped over a hefty dictionary that was known to play old rebel songs, but he caught his balance before toppling to the floor. I held my breath, but the book was heftier than he was, so the cover stayed put. All I needed now was to find myself in a situation where I had to explain why a book on my floor was singing "The Bold Fenian Men."

Not that it would matter now. Surely, he'd seen my mattress floating in midair?

"Sorry," he said yet again, stepping around the dictionary, an arm curled around his stomach.

"I-I'm sorry," I stammered back. What a feckin' poetic lot we were. I took a deep breath in an attempt to douse the wind rushing through my insides, begging to lift me. "I was having a nightmare."

"Figured," he mumbled, sidestepping a bucket that I'd forgotten to empty today. He didn't mention the mattress, and I wasn't going to bring it up.

As the sleep and the dream drifted away from me, Finbar squawked and flew back to his roost. A moment later, he returned and dropped a shiny half crown in my lap.

"Jaysus," I croaked, my throat dry and scratchy from my nightly screams. "Ríona'll be cross you've been stealing, j'know?"

"What … What is it?" Aidan asked, still turned toward my door.

I looked at him. Maybe there was more curiosity to him than I'd first thought. But if he wouldn't tell us his secrets, I wouldn't tell him ours, not levitating mattresses, or money-growing plants, or anything.

"Just a gift from Finny," I said, flipping the coin and catching it in my palm. "Go on, Finny, show him your treasures."

Finbar squeaked excitedly and hopped across my bed before taking off for his roost again. Aidan only stared after him.

I crawled out of bed and went to flip the switch near the door, bringing to life the old wooden chandelier kitted out with bare light bulbs that buzzed softly. I shook out my arms. That sometimes helped to stop the incessant fluttering in my veins.

"He wants to show you his things," I prompted Aidan.

Hesitating for only a moment, Aidan walked over to Finbar's door. Without having to ask what it was for, he carefully, still nursing his stomach, climbed on top of the wooden trunk turned up on its end to peer inside Finbar's nest.

Finbar squeaked again, something shiny in his beak. I couldn't tell what it was from across the room, but I figured I'd let them have this moment. Aidan was clearly terrified of my sweet Finny, and he had no reason to be.

"He's got all kinds of junk in there—"

"Junk!" I exclaimed. "Feckin' junk, like?"

"Junk!" Finbar repeated, his squawk as indignant as my own.

Aidan grinned, the first natural smile I'd seen on his face since he'd gotten here. "Sorry, I just meant … There's a lot of stuff in here. Even the nest … What's it made out of?

"Whatever Finbar found lying around. He'd have used moss and feathers, bits of my clothes and Faolan's fur for the bedding, and harder things for the foundation. Sticks, roots—"

"Is that a-a *bone*?" Aidan screeched.

"Yes, mice probably, j'know? He's a most resourceful little thing," I said proudly.

"That's … That's disgusting!" Aidan said, wrinkling his nose.

"Well, I think that's a matter of opinion!" I snapped. "After all, are we humans any different?" I gestured toward the castle walls.

Aidan narrowed his gaze at me and jumped down from Finbar's roost. "What do you mean?"

I gestured at the wall again.

Aidan tentatively stepped toward it. "I don't get it," he said, rubbing a palm over the medieval mortar.

"They used all kinds of things to build a castle like this." I walked to the window beside Finbar's roost — I knew these walls better than I knew most things — and pointed to a particularly large clump of brown twig-like things stuck in the wall.

"What is it?" Aidan asked, peering closer and running his fingers over it.

"That bit's straw. And animal blood."

"*What?*" he cried, drawing his hand back like he'd been burned.

"There's some horse hair in there, too, Dad reckons."

"Okay, that *is* more disgusting than your bird's nest," he said, rubbing his hands on the pair of Dad's trousers Moira had given him to sleep in.

"Pretend all you want," I said, strolling back to my bed, absolutely buzzing, "but something tells me you're not so different either."

His head jerked around so he could stare at me. "What's that supposed to mean?"

I kept my gaze level on him, fighting hard to keep my limbs still. "What was that thing in the water, Aidan?"

He gulped, and I wondered if he knew he was rubbing his forehead with the back of his hand. We all had our nervous tells, and I already knew his.

"Aidan," I said again.

"Aidan! Aidan!" Finbar squawked, swooping down from his roost to land on Aidan's shoulder.

The boy jumped, and then closed his eyes as if to settle himself into the feeling of a crow's talons clutching his shoulder.

"You wouldn't believe me if I told you," he whispered at long last.

"You don't know that."

"Bríd?" Moira stood in the doorway, a steaming mug in her hand, Ríona peeking over her shoulder. "Are you okay?" Moira's protective gaze was hard on Aidan, and I could see her mind going a mile a minute as she stalked to join me beside my bed.

"Yes, fine," I said, annoyed at our conversation being interrupted. I'd rather thought I could've ground down this boy's last reserve and gotten the truth out of him.

"We heard you making a fuss," Moira explained, "but Faolan slept soundly, so we didn't think it could be any danger. We thought we'd nip down and make you some tea first." She glanced at Aidan again. I was sure she didn't notice just how often her glance slid to him. And it wasn't always a defensive measure. Sometimes she looked at him curiously, sometimes admiringly, and sometimes her gaze slid up and down him like she kept discovering little details she'd never seen before. The last time I could remember Moira paying anyone that special attention was when we were twelve.

She'd had a thing for Brian Brennan then. I didn't know that from her own confession, of course — Moira had never been that kind of person. But she'd looked, glanced, paid an awful lot of attention, like she was now, and she'd even let him win in a foot race once. It had been clear as day to anyone watching that she had a crush. Even me, at twelve.

But Moira was the motherly one. The one who took care of us. Who would love us no matter what we did. And I knew that. So when Brian Brennan had pulled my braids and pushed me on the swing on the playground out the back of the school, I'd let him be the very first person to kiss me. With Ríona and Moira and half the children in Ballyconneely running around us. Even at twelve, I'd known I'd hurt Moira in a way that we would never speak of. But for some reason, that had only made me madder. Because the boys would continue to pull my braids and follow me around the playground and tell me I was pretty, and sometimes the only way to deal with the attention, to control it, was to bring it down upon myself. That way, at least, I was the one in power.

Ríona nudged Moira, and I watched as Moira's green gaze snapped away from Aidan and back to me. She had beautiful eyes, really striking, but you couldn't even attempt to tell her that. Sometimes I wondered if she'd know better how to love herself if Brian Brennan hadn't kissed me with those very green eyes watching. "Here," she said, blinking quickly. "Here you are. And we brought the spoon," she added as Ríona proffered the tarnished little teaspoon that made everything taste of sugar.

Ríona's gaze darted to Moira's face, and Moira's cheeks reddened. "I mean — a spoon," she amended quickly, her eyes going once again to our guest.

But I was about ready to tell Aidan that this teaspoon had the power to make anything taste of sugar. I wanted to tell him that that meant *anything.* That it was one of the earlier curios, and that as children we'd once tested it on oats and then broccoli and increasingly more disgusting things until Moira had been actually spooning up clumps of Bó's hay with glee. Because I thought, just maybe, if I told him that, he would share his secrets with us.

"Thank you," I said, carefully taking the tea from Moira and sitting down on my bed. Moira watched me closely, as I'd intended. My veins thrummed with a strong current, as they always did, but I breathed deeply and moved deliberately, forcing Moira to see that I was serious. "Aidan was actually just about to share something."

Moira and Ríona looked between us.

"What was the thing that attacked me, Aidan?" I asked carefully.

His gaze was on the floor, probably to avoid my sisters' perplexed stares.

"Aidan?" Moira whispered plaintively.

His arm went around his midsection, as if the memory of the monster was enough to make his wound ache anew. But he didn't complain. He never complained. Who was this boy who would sacrifice himself for strangers and give up no word of complaint?

At long last, he let his arm drop to his side, and the breath left him, his shoulders collapsing. "It's called a kelpie."

The room was silent, and even Finbar seemed to need a moment to collect his thoughts. "Kelpie," he squeaked a few moments later.

"What's a kelpie?" Moira asked, her gaze darting between us all, like she was the odd one out on some great joke.

Ríona and I shrugged, and Aidan looked up at long last.

"It's a barbaric, violent shape-shifter known to appear as a horse for the sole purpose of drowning its prey."

The room fell silent again, and this time even Finbar was speechless.

"Are you joking?" Moira asked at long last.

"I'm not," Aidan said, his face clear evidence of that. "Once ensnared, there's little a human can do to get away. You were lucky to escape. A kelpie is a predator above all else."

"Predit! Predit!" Finbar said, shaking his head as he struggled to repeat the word.

"God, you don't really … believe all that, do you?" Moira said, her eyes on Aidan.

"I do," I said.

All heads, human and avian, snapped to me.

"I do, because there are things around here that we can't explain."

"Brí," Moira said in a warning tone.

"There are things here, Aidan, that we don't understand, but we've just come to accept them because there's nothing else to do."

Aidan took a step forward, concern etched on his face, and I knew he was thinking of the mattress. Ríona's eyes were wide.

"Objects, animals that can do impossible things—"

"Bríd!" Moira yelled.

"Like this spoon." I shook it at him madly. "It makes everything taste of—"

"Bríd, *don't*!" Moira screamed. She was on top of me, shaking me angrily before I could get my thoughts back on track. "She's mad," Moira said, releasing me and bearing down on Aidan. "You need to leave. Now."

She had him at the door and was nearly pushing him down the stairs before he could cry, "Leave?"

A strangled shriek of frustration cut him off. Moira froze.

Ríona stood in the middle of the room, her tall frame shaking, her curls dancing around her shoulders with the effort of that one sound.

Aidan stared at her. I closed my eyes. It was so easy for Moira and me to do this — to get at one another, forget we were in this life together — with poor Ríona stuck in the middle. Always stuck in the middle.

I took a deep breath and watched the fight simultaneously drain out of Moira, too.

"He doesn't have to leave," Moira said at long last, her eyes on Ríona. "He just has to go downstairs … for now."

Ríona nodded in unison with Aidan, who was frantically bobbing his head and nearly tripping down the stairs in his haste to obey and not be tossed outside in the middle of the night. Or maybe it was haste to get away from us.

The three of us just stood there, three points on a wonky triangle, as the energy fizzled between us.

I was sure we'd just learned something very real. But I thought maybe we'd missed the most important question of all. And that wasn't what, exactly, a kelpie was. But how Aidan knew about it at all.

roghnú nádúrtha
NATURAL SELECTION

aidan

I wasn't sure why I told them except that I was scared. And I didn't want to be alone anymore. And there was something about them … I was pretty sure I hadn't been wrong about the levitating girl after all.

The pillow beneath my head felt and smelled older than the sea, but that would only have been a problem if I could actually sleep. As it was, my stomach was aching, and my mind was racing, yet I couldn't concentrate. There was a soft muffled murmur, and I assumed the girls were continuing their fight upstairs, but it invaded my brain down here like it was coming from the very walls. I couldn't concentrate on the things I needed to concentrate on.

Like the fact that there was no telling if Rory was still in Ireland, and if he was, I had all of Ireland to search.

If he wasn't … Well, I had no way of getting home.

With not a cent to my name, not a shoe or a hair brush, and not a

single explanation for the state I was in, I was well and truly screwed.

So it had seemed like the best idea at the time to tell the girls about the kelpie. Or maybe I'd just wanted to feel connected to someone again. For the first time in … well, I didn't know how long. I truly didn't. And I didn't know how I would find out. In that moment, it hadn't mattered. I'd only wanted to share something with another person, another strange, otherworldly person, find understanding, even if it was about something so horrible.

I'd known it as soon as I'd seen it down there on the beach. Kelpies weren't unheard of around this area, but they'd mostly been confined to the wilds of mountain lochs by simple natural selection. But where they did come into contact with people, only death followed.

The embers of the dying fire glowed painfully on my eyes, but I couldn't close them. Sleep felt as unnatural now, with everything thrumming through me, as my coat had once felt.

It had been pure chance that I'd been sitting there on the beach, in the clothes I'd found on the clothesline, when one of the sisters had begun to scream. Pure chance. Hadn't it been?

I'd felt the yearning, the need, early that morning. To change, to come back. And then to get away from this land.

Things had been churning for a while now, an energy rippling through the water, the feeling of things going wrong, going awry, but it hadn't been until that morning that the urge had rushed through my veins like my very blood was pushing, pulling, coaxing me onto the pebbled beach. The water had suddenly felt like suffocation.

But since I'd stepped foot on land, I couldn't feel it anymore, that certainty that something was wrong.

So I'd been wandering all day, seeing what I could, trying to make sense of it all, and I'd seen several things. This place wasn't as quiet, as ordinary, as it looked. I'd only returned to sit on the beach and wonder what was happening, why I'd come to shore, if I'd been tricked somehow … when the kelpie had appeared.

But I hadn't told the girls any of that. Or that they should've been terrified that I hadn't managed to injure the kelpie — only to scare it away.

For now.

But maybe it was time I did tell them. Because there was something about this place — these girls — that told me the castle was still as good a defense mechanism as it had probably been centuries ago. I just couldn't figure out why. Bríd had been about to tell me, to explain what I'd seen her do in her sleep, I was sure of it. But I didn't need her to spill their secrets to know that their presence here by the sea, in a half-sentient castle, was no coincidence.

foighne

PATIENCE

l o u i s

They weren't in the village at all that day. Conry would have known. And I didn't know how else to find them.

There was nothing for it. I'd have to bide my time on the bloody pig farm and play my part to the best of my ability.

Besides, I had less than a week until Lúnasa. And they were eighteen now. That was all that mattered. If I could make my move on the first of August, I'd be at my strongest, and everything would go according to plan.

If I could only get out of shoveling pig shit until then.

No bother. When Medb rewarded me, it would all be worth it.

I looked down at the triskele newly engraved in my skin.

Wouldn't it all be worth it?

coirceog
THE HIVE

moira

Bó snorted beneath my palm, so I gave her a good scratch high on her forehead and between her ears. She was moody today, like any mare is known to get now and again, but I knew her scratchy spot and just how to appease her. Time.

She had the run of the countryside, and plenty of neighboring horses to socialize with, but the true test of her heart was time. Time for her to get used to you. Time to watch one another and feel one another and understand one another. So I made it a habit to just sit with her, gently stroking her gray coat, or brushing her to the tune of the lullabies Mam used to sing us, which were somehow still lodged in my brain. "Sweet Bó," I murmured.

Calling my new gray Connemara "Bó," which is the Irish word for "cow," had seemed quite clever at five years old. That was when Dad had bought her off a farmer up in Clifden and given her to me. He'd

gotten her for cheap, as she'd already been nearly twenty at the time. Dad said the farmer had tried to talk him out of it — "your little girl won't want an old beast like this" — but I hadn't minded. Bríd had already found Finbar at the time, and Faolan, meant to be the family dog, had already become Ríona's shadow. I'd been feeling lonely, I suppose, and Dad had noticed. He noticed things like that. Like the way I'd always gravitated toward the horses in the fields along the lane into the village. They felt special to me, and so when I'd run outside and found an old spotted mare in our east field, I'd nearly fainted with happiness.

And she was still one of my favorite creatures in the world.

I was humming softly to her when she lifted her head in surprise. Looking over my shoulder, I found Aidan strolling across the bailey toward us. He was still moving a bit stiffly, but his hands were in the pockets of a pair of Dad's work jeans, and he looked every part the culchie with a red-and-blue plaid shirt from the depths of Dad's dresser.

Bó danced backward, and her ears fell flat against her head. Aidan paused a few steps away from me, eying Bó carefully. He'd clearly learned his lesson about animals that lived on the rustyback hill.

I gave him a small smile. "Tell her she's queen, and she'll deign to let you reside in her presence."

He quirked a brow at me.

I shrugged. "It's your life."

"Okay." He looked at Bó. "You are queen, of this castle, and this hill, and all you can see. Long may you reign. May I talk to your mistress now?"

Bó snorted, clearly not impressed by this charade, but she let her ears prick up, apparently finding no threat in this boy. I, despite all my natural defenses and warnings from my dad, felt the same. *Keep to the castle, and the castle will take care of you.* I'd abided by his one rule well, but he certainly hadn't been betting on us opening the castle up to outside forces. Like boys.

"Did you need something?" I asked. I'd hardly seen my sisters all morning, with this day being what it was, and after last night. With tempers still sore, the three of us had scattered to the wind, and that had probably left Aidan to fend for himself.

"Kind of," he said, rubbing a hand along his jaw.

"You say that a lot." Bó had stepped back up to me, and I let her head slide under my palm. At just over fourteen hands tall, she was a small thing to me now, though I remembered the days when we'd been of a height to one another.

"Do I?" Aidan asked, reaching out a hand to touch Bó's side.

"I can't say I've known you long enough to make a true judgment call, but from what I've heard … "

"Well, I guess I'm a bit shaken up," he admitted. "I've never been in a castle before." He looked around at the crumbling curtain wall that would make a sorry excuse for a defense these days. "This is actually my first time outside the U.S. Sort of."

"There you go again." I smiled so he'd know I wasn't still in the angry, fiery fit I'd been in last night.

He smiled back. "You're right. I'm finding it hard to make decisions these days. Which is one of the things I wanted to talk to you about."

"Oh?"

"I was wondering if it would be okay with you if I stayed a little longer." He fiddled with the right sleeve of Dad's shirt, which was a few sizes too big on him. "I just need to get a plan together, for how I'm going to find my family, and … hope my stomach heals up a bit and … Well, I guess I'd forgotten how much it rains in Ireland. A roof is kind of useful."

I laughed for real that time. The grass was still wet from that morning's shower, and as normal and reassuring as it usually felt, today it felt like the Earth's tears were soaking into my socks and I didn't know whether to feel irritation or go on and cry as well.

"Arah, I think we can share the castle a little longer," I said quietly.

Aidan looked at me, if not in surprise, then at least with apprehensive appreciation.

"If you have the guts to risk a repeat of last night," I added quietly.

He laughed. "That's not the scariest thing I've been through, not by a long shot."

"Well, you didn't see the bats. The bats really kick it up a notch."

I thought I was doing a fairly good job at this joking and jibing, but his eyes were studying me far too intensely. After I was positive he'd had enough time to memorize the map of freckles on my face, he asked, "Are you all right?"

Bó nudged my hand again, her mood returning in one lightly stomping foot. She had never had to duel a boy for my attention before.

"Today's our birthday," I said. "Me and my sisters."

Surprise appeared on Aidan's face. "Really?"

I nodded and tucked my hair behind my ears. It'd been years since I'd worn it in anything but a bob — a haphazard bob chopped away by Ríona whenever the length began to annoy me. Every time I touched it, I felt myself wishing I looked just a little more like either one of my sisters.

"All of you?" Aidan asked carefully.

I nodded again, silently daring him to question the probability of us actually sharing a birthday. Luckily, he didn't, because I would have fought anyone who dared to. The need to protect my sisters was a force so ingrained in my bones that sometimes it felt like I'd die if I was parted from them. And the feeling had been growing ever stronger lately. So strong, sometimes it felt like that need extended beyond my sisters — beyond Dad and Bó, even. To the ground beneath my feet, and the sea reaching up the hill to me, like a baby to its mother.

It was stupid, but sometimes the need to protect was so strong, it hurt. It had only been two days ago that it had finally brought me to tears.

The night before Bríd had been attacked by the kelpie — or whatever it was — I'd had that feeling in my bones. The feeling that I needed to stop bad things from happening. It had hurt so much that I'd finally crawled out of bed just before dawn and called Bó into the bailey. She'd let me climb onto her back, and we'd raced down the beach through the surf, my tears flowing freely and falling, falling, falling, mixing into the sea.

I felt like crying all over again.

Not talking to my sisters all day was clearly taking its toll on me. I needed to talk to someone, and Bó was in a mood.

"Does your birthday make you sad?" Aidan asked softly.

My sisters and I may not have been biologically related, but we were Mam and Dad's triplets all the same, the three of us taking that inexorable step forward in life every July 21. And this year, we were eighteen. Without Dad there to see it.

"Just this one," I whispered, shrugging one shoulder. "We're eighteen today."

"Ah," Aidan said knowingly. "Eighteen. Yeah, that's a tough one. You're practically over the hill now."

I smiled in spite of myself. "It's not that. It's just … our dad doesn't usually miss our birthday. And this is a big one."

"Where is he?"

"If I knew, I wouldn't be so worried."

"Is … Is he missing?" Aidan asked.

"He's just … on an extended business trip," I replied carefully. "Though he hasn't bothered with telling us he's been delayed."

"He hasn't called?"

"That's not his style. In fact, I'll probably be less upset if it turns out he's actually been maimed and is lying in a ditch somewhere."

He looked sideways at me, but I think the tears sparkling in my eyes belied my rough words. "What about your mom?"

"She died when we were little."

"Oh." Aidan rubbed the back of his neck. "I'm sorry."

Twisting my lips to the side, I blinked back tears and stared hard at Bó. The only sound was the far-off crash of waves on the beach, and the soft snap of Bó ripping grass out of the earth. Sometimes when I stood here, in the shadow of the castle, the great structure felt like a mother, the only thing we had taking care of us. And that made me mad. I didn't want a mother made of stone. I wanted the flesh and blood one who'd been taken from us.

No, I couldn't go down this road, not today…

"Are you hungry?" I asked, turning quickly on my heel. There it was again, that instinct to nurture.

Aidan jumped to catch up with me as I strode into the kitchen garden. "Um, a little," he said sheepishly.

Slipping out of my shoes, I went to the fridge. "Have a seat," I said, waving vaguely at the kitchen table. "Let me see what we have lying around."

My mistake only became apparent when Aidan yelped. "What the—"

I turned in time to see him jump out of a chair. The wooden chair at the end of the table. One of the strangest curios in the castle. And I'd let him stumble right into it. I pressed my eyes closed. Anyone who sat in that chair was overcome with a tickling sensation, almost as if the chair were trying to shoo you away. The tickling chair. That's what Dad called it. But that's not what I called it in my head.

To me, it was Mam's chair. That had always been her spot when we settled down to dinner, and shortly after she died is when the chair's strange antics started up.

Aidan's round eyes turned to me, as if to ask a question he was afraid to say out loud.

Shaking my head, I took a deep breath. There was no point hiding anything from him any longer. What Bríd had managed to get out last night before I'd gone nuclear would be enough for him to be asking questions — even if only in his head. I'd already said he could stay a little longer, and there wasn't much longer we could hold out without the secrets of the castle slipping out. Not that we'd ever had to try before.

"You can't sit there," I said simply.

Aidan stared at me.

"Look, that's what Bríd meant. Last night. About strange things in the castle we can't explain."

Aidan gaped at the chair.

"Come here." I went to the door of the kitchen and waited to see if he'd follow. He did.

The kitchen was attached to the tower house at its base, and I led him through to the thick-walled room at the very bottom of the tower. We called it a storage room, but it was more like a trash heap. Only a corner was cleared out and done up with hay for the odd night when Bó spooked at the high winds or there was the rare lightning. That wasn't the corner I moved toward now.

The buzzing was discernible even from across the room. I climbed over useless curios and broken furniture and the dust and debris of centuries to the giant stone urn in the far corner. Aidan was just behind me. When he hopped down from the old wooden table with a shattered leg, he landed very close to me. There was hardly any room for him to move away.

As I lifted the heavy lid of the urn, I watched his face.

His brown eyes grew round as the musical hum surrounded us. He didn't back away. He couldn't. Not with us pressed against the wall and the detritus of the castle. A flash of fear faded away to fascination, which made his eyes sparkle in a way that hit me in the gut and made me want to protect him, too.

A thousand bees lived inside this urn, all buzzing, living, working in a hive the size of a small dog. And Aidan was the first person outside our family who had ever seen it.

"Where did you … What is it?" he asked in a stutter.

"It just appeared one night a few years ago," I said, my eyes still on his face. His features were going through such a gamut of emotions, and I was afraid if I looked away, it would stick on the wrong one — disgust. Or fear. Of the bees. Of the castle. Of me.

"What do you mean it just appeared?" He looked at me, and I quickly looked down at the bees.

"That happens," I said softly. Embarrassment rushed through me, and I bent to put the urn lid on the floor — which conveniently turned my face from him. "Here in the castle. The hive appeared in Bríd's room, but she stuffed them down here to drown out the buzzing."

When I stood up, he was still looking at me, and I let my eyes fall back to the urn and the eternal business going on inside it.

A moment later, his laugh made me look up again. God, he was beautiful. His hair was dark, and he had one of those smiles that grew slow and steady until it swallowed his whole face and yours, too, and your heart, and the room, and the whole wide world and suddenly life felt a lot more like a good dream you didn't want to wake up from.

"So," he said, shaking his head, "in addition to a chair that tickles unwanted sitters, you have an unlimited supply of honey?"

I shook my head. "Not quite." I stuck my finger inside and Aidan lunged forward to stop me, but I smiled at him. "They won't hurt me."

Dipping a finger inside the hive, I gently felt around for the honeycomb and swiped at it. When I brought my hand out, a glittering, aromatic golden goo dripped down into my palm. It shone metallic, like liquid gold.

"That's not honey," he said.

I shook my head and held my finger out. "Better."

He stared at my finger for a moment, and I realized it looked as though I meant for him to lick it right off my pointer. My cheeks went hot, but he reached out and touched his finger to mine.

I stuck my finger in my mouth to show him what to do, and the sweet taste coated my tongue.

Before bringing it to his lips, he narrowed his eyes at me. "I'm going to wait a sec. See that you make it. Verify this isn't poison."

I smiled. "Exactly what century do you think you stumbled into here?"

His face sobered. "I don't know," he said softly.

Ignoring his strange reply, I prompted him with a "Mmm."

Finally, he brought his finger to his lips. The grin reappeared on his face. "Chocolate?"

I tried to grin back, but it slipped. He wasn't disgusted or afraid or even confused. And that scared me more than any sea monster could. Who was this boy?

"You're awfully modest about owning a hive of magic bees," he said, licking his finger clean.

I picked at a loose thread in the skirt of my dress. "It's just … unsettling," I whispered.

"What is?"

"Them buzzing around, uselessly, for eternity. Not knowing what they're doing. It isn't honey." At first, we'd thought it was liquid gold. The discovery that it wasn't had dampened Dad's mood for some three months. "I don't know what it is. But it isn't natural."

"Natural?" Aidan repeated. He rested one hand on the edge of the urn, and I knew from years of experience that you could feel the steady thrum through the stone with your palm pressed against it like that. "'Natural' is a word people use to describe the things they understand and shut out what they don't. When in reality, there's far more that's innate to this world than we'll ever understand."

The bees buzzed, and the castle's beams above us sighed, and I knew I had to ask.

"Aidan," I said, and I looked into his eyes, willing myself not to chicken out and look away. "You know about this stuff ... Stuff like our curios, and that kelpie monster, and who knows what else. Who are you?"

He let his hand fall. "I'm just Aidan." He cleared his throat. "And you," he said, his voice changing as he rocked back on his heels and folded his arms across his chest. "Are you trying to tell me that a girl who has a literal unlimited supply of chocolate gold could possibly be unhappy on her birthday?"

Stooping, I struggled to lift the urn's lid off the floor, but Aidan grabbed it from me, easily sliding it back into place.

The bees disappeared, their gentle hum instantly muffled.

rúin na taoisigh
SECRETS OF CHIEFTAINS

ríona

"It's a good thing we don't have any visitors," Bríd huffed, "because if we did, I'd die of embarrassment when they saw *this* is what we're doing for our eighteenth. Some feckin' rager, girls." Even Finbar was nodding off on Bríd's shoulder. I looked at Aidan. "I mean, *other* visitors, like," Bríd added quickly.

"Stop being thick," Moira said, but her tone was lighter than usual. I sensed it was down to our guest's presence — Moira's feelings, her thoughts, they weren't pushing at me like usual. They seemed reserved, relaxed. Content. Her fingers were gentle and slow as she braided my hair for bed.

She was even wearing the rack of red deer antlers on her head, which she never did in front of other people. They were a favorite of hers, as far as her interest in the curios went. They'd appeared in her room just after our mother had died, but they'd been much too big for

us then. Still, we'd figured them out pretty quickly — they bestowed a sense of power upon the wearer.

"It's not a real power," Bríd had yelled at Moira more than once, *"like everything else from this feckin' pile of rubbish!"* She said Moira only liked the antlers for the power trip. But I didn't think that was it. More than anything, what I always felt from Moira was fear. Fear for us, for our animals, for our dad, for creatures and people we didn't even know. And all that worry had to be tiring. I figured the antlers gave her a sense, just for a little while, of being in control. Of having the power to protect us.

In any event, the boy, Aidan, hadn't looked twice at the antlers since I'd come in, so I suspected Moira had revealed more than a few of our secrets to him. Which was precisely what I'd unsuccessfully attempted to accomplish last night.

"We can't go into the village for a week at least," Bríd said, interrupting my thoughts, annoyance undulating off of her with her usual energy. "People'll be bound to ask how we spent our birthday, and I can't tell them about this sad little affair." *Her* feelings, unlike Moira's, were pressing me just as usual. She had a boundless energy unlike many people I'd felt before, and it felt especially combative today for being pent up in a life she didn't dream was right for herself. That was the problem with Bríd, I thought. Our life never lived up to her dreams. Not that I knew what happened in her dreams. She sometimes shared, but I didn't think she told the truth.

"Then make something up," Moira suggested to Bríd. "Isn't that what you love to do, anyway? Where is it you told Stephen Waldron you were going working next summer? Greece, was it?"

Bríd ignored her and flopped backward on the couch she had to herself. Finbar squawked and flew into the air to avoid being flattened by his mistress. Little pricks of indignation poked at me, as Finbar's feelings always felt — tiny, and usually in line with Bríd's. Even with the rustyback hill growing a little more crowded than usual, it was still much easier for me to deal with here than in a crowded place like the village.

Faolan was asleep at my feet, as demure as ever, and the only other being in the room to press at my consciousness was Aidan. And from him, I felt the same frantic energy so mismatched to his outlying demeanor. As if he had two personalities, and we could only see one. But I was getting a bit used to it, to be honest, like radio static playing in the background. He'd been a wonderful addition to the dinner table, and Moira had made us *adalu* for dinner, a dish of beans and corn that had been a favorite of Mam's, along with my own favorite — roasted plantains. If my sisters would only have stopped squabbling, it would have been a sort of pleasant scene.

Aidan was wandering around behind the couches now, stopping to gaze at the few photos that sat in the recessed wells of the mullioned windows. Through the thick glass, the bats were visible flitting through the night, but Aidan didn't seem to notice. When he paused in front of a photo of our mother, I watched him. He bent close and studied it for a long time. It was a shot of our mother holding Bríd on her lap as they sat on a big rock on the rustyback hill, the tiny green plants it was named for poking out of the cracks in the rock.

People said I looked like her, but it was hard to tell from the handful of pictures we had of her. All our neighbors truly meant when they remarked on it was that I had the dark springy hair and brown skin that meant I could've been the biological child of our mother — whose parents had come from Nigeria to settle in Scotland — and our father — whose ancestors had lived in various corners of Ireland — while my sisters didn't.

When he turned around, Aidan came straight back to the corner of the living room where we lounged around the fire. "So," he said brightly, "how can three girls who live in a magic castle look *this* bored on their eighteenth birthday?"

"See?" Bríd scoffed at Moira. "Even our single party guest thinks we're dry shites!"

A crack of thunder shook the old windows, and we all looked outside. Everyone except Aidan.

"Hey, do you have any of those curio things that could help me?" Aidan asked, brightening even more as he turned to Moira. He may have been accustomed to storms, but we were not. It was a rare day that found thunder and lightning in Ireland. We were used to the mild weather wrought by our corner of the Atlantic, but Mother Nature seemed to have other ideas for us this summer. "Help me find my brother, I mean," Aidan added, when we failed to gather our thoughts as a bolt of lightning lit up the room. He stepped into the center of the couches, and the flames danced behind him.

"Ah." Bríd sighed. "So you haven't quite grasped the fact that this castle has never fabricated something that's actually of any use here in the real world."

Not true, I thought darkly. Faolan rolled over and scooted away from me. He hated when I disturbed his evening naps. I grasped the half crown in the pocket of my trousers.

Moira glared at Bríd as she gently turned my head back toward her to tie off the last braid. "That may be partially true, but that's not to say *we* can't help you," she told Aidan.

"Yeah, like we're much more use than this place," Bríd said, thumping an arm against the couch. "We haven't got a thing to our name that could actually help you in any way." She sat up. "You want a shoe that'll silence your steps? Just the one, of course, can't be *too* useful now."

"*You* lost the other one!" Moira snapped.

"Or how about a wolf-dog who'll only obey silent commands?" Bríd went on, nodding at Faolan. I thought that was a low blow, but there was no point arguing with her. I only rolled my eyes.

"How 'bout a pillow that whispers secrets in your ear all night if you try to use it?" She grabbed the pillow off the couch beside her and hurled it at Aidan.

He managed to grab it just before it went sailing into the fire. Recognition came over his face as the soft murmuring filled Bríd's silence. I hadn't even noticed it. It was so much background noise to me now.

Aidan laughed out loud. "*This* is where all the whispering was coming from last night?" he nearly shouted. "It kept me up half the night!"

I smiled. I liked a person who found the curios as entertaining as I did.

"What?" Bríd said with mock astonishment. "Don't you want to hear hundreds of years' worth of dead people's secrets instead of sleeping? Wouldn't that be so *useful?*"

"God, Bríd, the whole world isn't meant to serve you!" Moira yelled, the antlers shaking on her head. "Can't something just *exist?*"

Finbar squawked at Moira, swooping low overhead. But Moira didn't even flinch. We were used to Finbar fighting Bríd's battles while she just glowered.

"Hold on," Aidan said, his enjoyment undiminished by my bickering sisters. "Did you purposely give me a pillow I couldn't sleep on?"

My head jerked up when I realized he'd found me out.

"To lower my defenses or something? To make me weak?" He was smiling, so I smiled back, ignoring Moira and Bríd's stares. They hadn't even figured that much out.

Of course I'd given him that particular pillow last night because I'd been hoping he'd unravel our secrets. This wasn't a normal boy. From the very start, I'd known that, his split feelings forever confounding me. I couldn't explain it, the way other people felt to me, but this was different. He was different.

Almost inhuman.

Brian Brennan liked to call me that. Not that I sought his company much anymore, but a childhood of harsh words can linger. And his certainly had. But for some reason, the way Aidan felt, especially here, in our inner sanctum, he made *inhuman* seem just a little better than the alternative.

And we'd been too long with these secrets. I hadn't known it until this boy had walked into our castle, but we wanted to let them out. Needed to.

Moira and Bríd were still looking at me, wondering, calculating, thinking things they'd never tell me but I would feel in my heart all the same.

"No!"

We all jumped.

Aidan had the whispering pillow pressed to his ear. "Say it isn't so! Teige Ó Flaithbheartaigh" — he butchered the name spectacularly — "stole a whole cart of chickens from his cousin upon failing to take back the castle. A whole cart!"

Moira and I laughed at his mock seriousness, and Finbar gave a mirthful caw in Bríd's stead. She clearly still wasn't sure if she wanted to give up quarreling with her sister for this. It was easier to feel sorry for oneself when fighting.

Undeterred by her sour expression, Aidan screwed up his face and asked, "Teige Ó Flaithbheartaigh?"

"That's not how you say it." Moira giggled, righting the antlers on her head. They'd slipped sideways. But Aidan pretended not to hear and pressed the pillow to his ear again, as if for more details. I knew well what it would sound like: a large group of people whispering, murmuring, and moving away and back as you strained to hear.

"And Friar John Smythe was booted from the castle in front of a full party for stealing away mead? It's an outrage!"

Even Bríd cracked a smile at that. Faolan raised his head, blinked at us, and lay back down with a sigh, determined to sleep through our fun.

"Who's going to be my leading lady?" Aidan asked theatrically, extending a hand like he was asking one of us to dance.

Holding the antlers to her head, Moira jumped to her feet on the couch. "Arah, I'll have a go!"

Aidan tossed her the pillow, then followed in its wake, jumping up onto the couch and pressing his ear to the side of the pillow opposite Moira. Her cheeks went pink, but I was surely the only one to notice, having been alerted by a frantic beating coming at me from her direction.

"Among the crumbling walls of the kitchen did Cathleen Walsh sit with her bag of belongings," Moira recited, her eyes closed as she listened to the otherworldly voices, "at the time and day prescribed by her friend and lover, Dermot O'Sullivan. Upon that rock did she fall asleep, still waiting. Upon that rock did her father find her come morning."

"Aw, no!" Bríd cried. "That's tragic, like!"

We'd heard these secrets all before, but we'd never paid them so much attention. They were made anew, riveting and tantalizing and entertaining, simply by Aidan's interest.

"Oh, but you'll like this one, Bríd," Moira said happily, and my heart felt lighter. They were friends again, as easy as that. "Conor O'Malley, son of Owen O'Malley, of the Mayo O'Malleys," Moira recited with a glint in her eye, giving special attention to the titles in that way the pillow tended to do, "was seen ravaging by ship in West Connacht. He took prizes from these very walls, curse him to the end. But would you know it? On the way to Aran, the riches of these walls went down with the thieving ship, and the soul of Conor O'Malley. The thick eejit!"

I was pretty sure that last bit was Moira's own addition.

"Let me have a go!" Bríd cried, jumping to her feet on her own couch. Moira tossed it over happily, and this time Aidan stayed put. A low rumbling of thunder sounded outside, this one much different than the cracks that made me jump. This slow, resounding sound felt the same as a low, rumbling growl in Faolan's throat.

"That poor shipwrecked soul found in East Bay," Bríd repeated after the pillow, her eyes screwed up at the ceiling. "Hang on… He was later seen? Sewn? Bean? Within these hallowed walls with Gráinne Ní Mháille, even during her marriage to Dónal an Chogaidh Ó Flaithbheartaigh, heir to the Ó Flaithbheartaigh title and future ruler of Iar Connacht!"

We all laughed uproariously. There was one story we knew by heart — that of the Pirate Queen. She'd always been a favorite of ours in storybooks, and in Dad's stories about her connection to the castle centuries ago. Of course, his stories had the ring of embellishment to them, but the pillow was telling the truth.

For all we knew, anyway.

"Ríona, hold this for a moment!" Bríd tossed the pillow to me and ran for the stairs. She reappeared only a moment later with the musical dictionary and plopped it down on the floor in front of the fire, opening it to a page full of G words. Old Irish music filled the air as Bríd grabbed the pillow back from me and launched it at Aidan.

"Here sat the Baron Athenry with his feet up, a warm drink, and the news that Teige Ó Flaithbheartaigh did burn and ravage sixteen villages along the border," he proclaimed, like a judge in a movie, the dictionary supplying his backing track as he imparted charges upon a long-ago villain.

The frenzied gale of their excitement was strong enough to make me feel lightheaded, but in a good way — like I thought it might feel to drink a bit too much wine.

"The paint applied by the workers hired by Sir Richard Clarence did cover the blood of a mistress," Moira cried, really getting into the part as the singing of the dictionary's current song crescendoed. "And upon her body did this castle rise again."

"Gross!" Aidan groaned. "That's messed up!"

"You Americans have feckin' weak stomachs." Bríd laughed. "You haven't heard the one about the bear yet."

It all had the air of a festival. A Shakespearean festival, though the tales were more sordid, and we the lowly players. That was what I was thinking when I saw it.

A door, next to the mullioned windows on the west wall.

It was simply there, where it hadn't been before.

Bríd saw my outstretched finger first. Her gaze followed where I pointed.

I approached it.

"What are you —?" Aidan's word faltered.

Moira was behind me by the time I ran a hand over the rough, dark wood of the door. It didn't match any of the other doors in the castle.

"Was … Was that always there?" Aidan asked, but the tone of his voice told me he knew the answer already. He did, after all, still hold in his hands the whispering pillow.

The hinges were a rusted orange, but there was no mistaking its age. Whether it had existed elsewhere before this moment, it had only been here mere seconds.

"That's not possible," Aidan murmured. "We're on the third

floor."

His definition of possible was about to change.

Bríd pushed in front of me and wrenched open the door.

My breath caught in my throat.

The room was dark and smelled of rotting old wood, but a single candle flickered in the corner, illuminating its contents. It was a wine cellar.

And despite our being on the third floor, and despite there being no room off this wall of the castle, there was a room now.

Aidan dashed to the mullioned window to look outside. But I knew what he'd see. Nothing. There would be nothing there as surely as this room was here.

Bríd stepped inside first, a giant smile on her face and Finbar on her shoulder. "Wine, girls!" she called, her voice muffled as she shuffled around inside. "Our fairy godmother has clearly been listening to my prayers!"

"Wine!" Finbar cried as they stepped back out, Bríd's arms positively full of clinking wine bottles.

"Let's get pissed!"

It took only one sip on Aidan's part for Moira to follow suit. They each held a bottle of their own, their fingers dusty from the old glass and their faces pink from the rush of excitement.

"Ríona?" Bríd asked, holding a whole bottle out to me.

Though she'd stolen sips of Dad's whisky a few times over the years, I'd never had so much as a sip. But there she stood with a dark crimson bottle held out to me, utter mirth in her eyes, on our eighteenth birthday.

Our eighteenth birthday, when our father had abandoned us, storms took over the coast, and we spilled all our secrets to a total stranger who'd walked out of the sea.

I grabbed the bottle.

"Whoa, there." Bríd laughed, stepping forward to pull the cork off for me with an old rusty tool she'd found in the wine cellar. Then I tipped it forward and lifted the end until the sweetly sour liquid ran down my throat.

It goes without saying that our portrayals of the past whispered by the pillow only became more dramatic from there.

"From this door did Brian Ó Flaith … Flaib … 'eartuh listen for the secrets to betray his cousin Murrough Ó Flabby Heart in order to gain the castle from the crown across the sea!" Aidan shouted, as if the very man stood before us and he'd betrayed us personally.

"Bloody English traitor!" Bríd nearly screamed, laughing just as loud.

"Richard Óg de Burgh, 2nd Earl of Ulster and 3rd Baron of Connacht, son of Walter de Burgh, 1st Earl of Ulster, 2nd Lord of Connacht … God!" Moira cried, pretending to wipe her brow. "I'm bored just repeating all that!"

"My turn!" Aidan cried, pulling the pillow from her. They had a little playful scuffle, and I wondered just how much they'd each had to drink. Their bottles sat beside one another on the floor, but I couldn't see how much was left of either.

Aidan cleared his throat. "Upon this very floor did Moira first set her eyes upon he who would become … "

I sucked in a breath, and my gaze flew to Moira. The pillow had never told us a secret of our own. But we'd relegated it to a pile of unused curios long ago. We'd probably grown considerably since it had last been used. And oftentimes growing considerably meant amassing considerable secrets.

I felt Moira's nerves vibrating in time with my own.

"First set her eyes upon he who would become the first to dethrone her from her own couch!" Aidan cried. With that, he shoved her hard, catching her at the very second before she would fall.

Moira squawked indignantly and grabbed the pillow from Aidan, only to bash him over the head with it. "You really had me going, you slag!"

"I saved you, Moira, first of her name, second of her sisters, third of her—"

"You don't get to play anymore!" Moira laughed, brushing her hair out of her eyes and steadying the antlers.

"Okay, okay, I'm sorry," Aidan said, covering his head with his arms to stop her assault. "No more improv."

"Yes, you best stick to the script," she retorted, letting the pillow hit him one more time before letting go.

He pressed it to his ear and took on a mock serious expression. It was all the more comical for the wine he'd consumed. He cleared his throat. "And upon a day dark and dreary, at this kitchen table, did Brian Doyle sign away his soul for those of his ruthless daughters!"

I was the first to interpret Aidan's smile correctly. It wasn't the goofy grin he'd used to tease Moira. It was a salacious smirk, entertained and intrigued.

Because he didn't know Brian Doyle was our father.

Bríd stopped laughing first. Then Moira.

"What did you say?" Bríd asked.

"Daughters!" Finbar squawked, cocking his head at Aidan from Bríd's shoulder.

Aidan looked around at our faces and stilled, letting the pillow fall from his ear. "It just said something about a Brian Doyle. Who's that?"

We stared at each other in silence.

Which probably made the knock sound all the louder.

Faolan reared up and let out a ferocious but stunned growl, still half-asleep.

But I didn't dare move. This moment felt like a brittle structure that would come tumbling down if I moved even an inch.

Somebody was at the door.

"Daughters!" Finbar squawked as there was another loud pounding below us.

"Do you think that's …?"

Bríd looked from Moira to me and back again.

We all flew into motion at once, dashing for the stairs. Moira was the first there, of course, even after throwing off the antlers, but we were hot on her heels, Faolan bringing up the rear to be near me. I didn't even turn around to see where Aidan was. I had to see Dad. He wouldn't have missed our birthday for anything but a good reason — or a horrible one. I felt the relief from both my sisters washing over me, and the refrain replayed in my head, though none of us spoke it: *He is okay. Dad is alive, and he is okay, and he is here.*

But something still felt wrong.

Something I couldn't decipher behind the relief and happiness and excitement pouring off my sisters as we tumbled down the stairs like some three-headed creature.

We bounded down the hallway on the ground floor as one, but as we turned the corner to the front hall, Bríd stopped abruptly. Moira and I were already at the door when she spoke:

"He wouldn't knock."

None of us moved.

The truth ricocheted between us, a three-pointed conundrum that didn't want to be solved. We'd have preferred to go on believing forever that it was Dad on the other side of that door. Because if it wasn't, that meant he wasn't here, he had missed our birthday completely, and he might not be safe. Probably *wasn't* safe. And, just as terrifying and unfamiliar, it meant there was a stranger on our doorstep.

The triangle formed by our bodies snapped into a straight line as Moira moved past me to the door and opened it.

A figure stood in the rain on the doorstep.

It wasn't Dad. It was an old woman.

She fell to her knees the moment she saw us.

an chead impíoch
THE FIRST SUPPLICANT

b r í d

She was bent like a tree near the sea, and her skin was white as paper. It fairly glowed, despite the lack of moonlight. She looked around us eagerly, as if looking for someone she knew. The rain pelted her sideways, but she didn't seem to notice.

"Can I help you?" Moira asked carefully. The woman was obviously in the wrong place, but something about her made me wonder if she was entirely all right. Did she need help? The wine was dulling my senses, and I felt my thoughts swirling sleepily. We were the only house for quite a walk in every direction, so if she'd gotten into some kind of trouble, we would be her only option. Yet she would have had to hike up the whole hill to get here …

The way her eyes gleamed and darted between us with an eerie interest set my teeth on edge. She seemed very sure that she was in exactly the right place for whatever she intended. And what kind of

errand would bring someone along in the night? Something dark and sinister, that's what. Finbar ruffled up his feathers, tickling my ear. He was uneasy, too. And *his* thoughts were unclouded by wine.

"Can I help you?" Moira repeated gently. I could see her need to help this woman taking shape. Of course, that, too, was probably exacerbated by the drink. Still, maybe this woman *did* need our help …

"Where is she?" the woman asked in a voice like an old door creaking shut.

We all stared at her. Even Faolan, whose fur was bristling at his nape.

The old woman's mouth hung open just a little as her dark eyes continued to bounce back and forth between us. Suddenly, she was on her feet and took a huge step forward, over the thick doorjamb.

Moira darted forward and closed the door halfway, preventing the woman's entrance.

"Where is she?" the woman asked again, wedging a muddy old boot in the door.

"Who? Who are you looking for?" Moira asked desperately, discreetly pressing all her weight against the door. Thankfully, her instinct to protect us came before whatever sympathy she had for this woman. For I didn't trust her yet. I stood behind Moira, ready to push, too, if need be.

"Frenzy," the old woman said, her eyes on me. "Is it you?" Her eyes slid to Finbar, and she cocked her head just slightly, like Finbar himself when he heard a strange sound. Then she shook her head.

"You're at the wrong house," I said, stumbling forward, courtesy of the wine, and gently adding my weight to the door.

The woman took issue with that and flung the door open, causing Moira and me to stumble backward. Finbar squawked and took flight, retreating to perch on a rusty old hook near the ceiling. Aidan jumped in front of us to close the door, but it was too late. The woman was in the hall.

Her jacket was soaking wet, but her clothes were neat and well-kept. Her gray hair fell stringy around her shoulders, but it, too, was cut straight and clean. She didn't look like someone who made a habit of roaming the countryside in the night. And now, she was moving with a shaky determination.

Faolan stood in front of us and growled as we regained our footing. "You need to leave," Aidan said, as if Faolan's throaty threat needed translation.

The woman's gaze locked on Faolan's yellow eyes, and her mouth tipped up in a smile.

"She's mad, like," I muttered to Moira.

"Maybe … Maybe she's just lost," Moira whispered back. "What else would she be doing out in the storm?" My sister looked to Aidan, as if for reassurance or advice or something else she needed in that moment, but he only shrugged back.

Moira bit her lip. Aidan must have noticed, because he gulped and stepped forward, taking in a deep breath as if to blow himself up into an intimidating figure. "Who are you looking for?" he asked in a voice a few pitches deeper than his usual one.

But the woman didn't seem to hear him. Her eyes had moved on from Faolan and were fixed on a new interest.

"It's you," the woman whispered at Ríona.

Faolan growled, planting himself in front of his girl. Ríona's hands shook where she clasped them in front of her.

"I can see it in your face and hear it in your silence," the woman said, and she fell to her knees right there in front of Faolan. "Oh, great queen!"

The rumble died in Faolan's throat, but he stood, fierce as ever, his golden eyes on the woman in front of him. Only, now, he seemed to be appraising her. Was she really no threat to us?

"Please," the woman said, grabbing Ríona's wrist. Still, Faolan didn't move, and I cursed him as I dashed to defend my sister.

"Don't touch her!" Moira shouted.

"I know you can heal that which you cause, Mo Bhanríon!" the woman cried. Her keen interest had turned to desperation, which was somehow worse as her thin fingers looped around Ríona's wrist.

"Let her go!" I yelled, but Moira beat me there. She pried the woman's hand off Ríona, who stepped backward, shaking like a leaf in a gale. Lightning lit up the corridor through the open door, throwing the woman's outline into a positively terrifying contrast.

Aidan grabbed the woman's other hand, and together, he and Moira tugged her toward the door. Still, Faolan didn't move. I slipped a protective arm around Ríona's back. Her shaking body rocked my own.

"The frenzy!" the woman wailed, thrashing out of Moira's grip. "I know it's in you! And I suffer so!"

Aidan grunted as the woman's elbow connected with his already injured middle. Apparently, she was quite the match for a pair of tipsy teenagers. "Come on—"

"I see things that aren't there," she said, ripping out of Aidan's grasp and latching back on to Ríona. "I hear things, too."

My skin grew warm, and I froze. What if she saw things like doors that weren't there yesterday and heard things like songs coming from books?

What if this woman was like us?

"You need to leave — *now*!" Moira yelled.

"I know you can make it stop!" the woman yelled louder. "They've told me so!"

"Who are 'they'?" I asked, but there was too much bluster around me for my words to be heard. I felt like Faolan now, watching, waiting, not ready to condemn this woman back out into the storm.

But Moira had on her fiercest, most protective look, and Aidan appeared ready to do her bidding. Together, they dragged the woman through the door and managed to get her to the little bridge over the Killeen River. I could see the Whitethorn and Blackthorn leaning ominously in the wind on either side of the woman's kneeling figure. Moira and Aidan ran back inside and together slammed the door as the woman continued to wail about a queen and the frenzy.

Moira slumped backward, her back pressed against the door. We stood there, frozen, as the woman's wailing went on for a few more minutes. Faolan stood at the door, gently pawing it, until all went silent.

"Is she gone?" Moira whispered after another few moments.

"I think so," Aidan said softly.

Moira heaved in a deep breath, and a single droplet slid down her cheek.

I thought she was crying, until she looked up.

Above her, water was trickling down the wall and dropping from the doorjamb, right onto her face. An ominous crack ran across the corner of the ceiling. A new one.

With a sputtering breath, Moira burst into tears.

"It's okay," I said quickly, "I'll get a bucket."

Before I could run for the kitchen, Moira shouted, "Let it fall to pieces for all I care! God, all of it!"

Ríona still stood shaking where I'd left her. But Moira didn't move to comfort her. She stood rigid, her face red and angry. Aidan lingered awkwardly behind us, clearly uncomfortable.

"Everything's fine," I said softly, hoping to soothe. "Nobody's hurt, j'know? And Dad will be home soon."

"Fine? *Fine?*" Moira shouted, her hands in fists. "First, you're attacked by a sea monster! Then, strange boys start appearing all around us, and now, it's terrifying vagrants with some kind of vendetta against Ríona! Meanwhile, the castle is literally falling down around us! Dad is *missing*, Bríd. He's not coming home. Absolutely nothing is *fine!*"

an comhartha
THE OMEN

ríona

The next morning dawned bright and cloudless, as if those in charge of such things were mocking us. Mocking the fear we'd slept with last night. For the first time, we'd secured the doors with chairs. And prayed to every spirit out there that Dad was being literal when he'd told us the castle would take care of us. That Mam's stories of Whitethorn and Blackthorn and faeries were less surreal than they felt. And yet …

At this kitchen table did Brian Doyle sign away his soul for those of his ruthless daughters.

What did it mean? It hung over us all, but we dared not speak of it. Because it wouldn't bring us any closer to the truth, but it would bring us all closer to the edge.

"We should've used the murder hole," Bríd said as we sat around the kitchen table, each of us nursing a cup of tea and a fry-up. Except

Aidan, who'd opted for just a plate of scrambled eggs.

"The what?" he asked now, his eyes wide. He was, so far, the only one of us who was dealing with the aftermath of wine without so much as a headache. I'd barely eaten any of my eggs. A heavy pall lay over me, as if my senses were still dulled like last night, only a thought or a feeling from one of the others nudging through to my brain every now and again.

"No, we should've called the guards," Moira said sternly, rubbing her forehead.

"The *what* hole?" Aidan repeated, his frenetic aura kicking it up a notch.

"And say what?" Bríd asked, ignoring him as she moved her fork aside so Finbar could hop onto the edge of her plate and dig his beak into a tiny glob of egg. "'There's an old woman here talking shite about a queen! No, she hasn't done anything wrong, besides being feckin' strange, like.'"

"Strange!" Finbar squealed.

"Well," Moira said with a huff, "that's—"

"Excuse me!" Aidan yelled. "Did you say you have a *murder hole*?"

We all looked at him. Even Faolan lifted his sleepy head to stare.

"Could ya not yell?" Bríd asked earnestly. "My head's wrecked, like."

"Sorry," Aidan mumbled. "If you could just update me on this murder thing … "

"Don't tell me ye don't have murder holes in America?" Bríd asked.

"They don't have castles in America, Bríd," Moira said, rolling her eyes.

"Well, lad, you're missing out. The *pol na mairbha* is a hole in the floor of the chapel, the ceiling of the front hall," Bríd explained, her lips tipping up into the first smile of the morning. She loved little more than messing with boys. "Once an enemy breached the castle door, you'd retreat to the next floor and dump scalding oil and tar and rocks and whatever else you could find through the murder hole. Honestly, I think everyone should have one."

Aidan gaped at her. "Do all the rooms in this place have secret doors and ways to kill people?"

Bríd shrugged. "Mostly."

"All right!" Moira said, a thunder cloud round her head as she stood up and grabbed her plate and Bríd's. Finbar squealed and took to the air as the plate was pulled out from beneath him. Moira's worry swung around the room like a dagger. "That's enough with the scary stories! We've all had enough of it!" Finbar settled on the edge of the hob, pecking at the remains in the frying pan. "Shoo!" Moira screeched, grimacing and touching her forehead again. Then she rounded on us. "All of you! Go outside and give Bó some clean water. The storm'll have turned hers to a dirty stew. Just … Just be careful. Keep watch around the place. I'll do the washing up."

We hadn't yet discussed the things Moira had yelled at us last night. Namely, that Dad wasn't coming home. And what, exactly, we were going to do about that. Nor had we discussed what the pillow had told us. If there was one thing the Irish were good at, it was talking nonstop while talking about nothing at all.

But I knew Moira would have opted to go see Bó herself if she hadn't been more eager to be alone. And I could feel her fear sharp as a knife, see it weighing her down, solid as my own. Besides, I knew as she retreated to do the washing, she would be devising a plan. And we needed a plan right about now. So I followed Bríd and Finbar outside the kitchen door without fuss. Faolan glanced up but only met my eyes and laid his head back down. I'd kept him in again last night, and he was sleepy now from all the whining and pawing at the door he'd done all night. And, of course, he was also giving me the cold shoulder. But I could handle it. It was the price I'd have to pay for keeping him safe.

Only Aidan stayed in the kitchen, standing to bring his own plate to the sink. And Moira didn't seem to mind.

Outside, the sun was so bright that I had to squint for a moment. Bríd was stomping through the grass, muttering and mumbling about Moira. Ducking under the laundry lines crisscrossing the kitchen garden, I let the unkempt grass tickle my shins as my mind wandered back to that woman from last night.

She'd terrified me thoroughly, but how much of that had been down to the wine and the time of night? Maybe she'd just gotten lost and was experiencing some mental issues. Should we have helped her?

"It's you," her words whispered inside my mind. I shivered in the bright sun. It was me she'd come for. I'd felt it, as clearly as if she'd come brandishing a sign with my name on it, before her eyes had ever fallen on me.

And she'd called me "queen."

The frenzy. That was what she'd said was in me. And what she suffered from, too. Was the frenzy what caused me to feel what other people were feeling, thinking, contemplating? Was it the frenzy that made words so difficult for me to speak? Was it the frenzy that caused strange things to happen in the castle?

"Jaysus, eighteen is feckin' horrible so far, *abi*?" Bríd grumbled, kicking at a tuft of grass. The ghost of a smile met my lips as Mam's voice slipped from Bríd, and I felt a little less strange. I didn't know what *the frenzy* was, but I did know who I was. *It's a beautiful day, abi?* Mam would've said if she was with us now. *Isn't it, girls?*

Bó was just inside the curtain wall, or what was left of it. The crevices were filled with the summer-green of the rustyback fern, and the last remaining flanking tower was nearly covered in it. Bó lingered near the longest grass growing at the base of the last tower. There would have been four at one time, one in each corner of the castle's curtain wall, part of the castle's outermost defense system. But our defense system was crumbling and nearly non-existent now — which was what had made last night so scary.

Bríd walked straight past Bó to the stairs of the flanking tower. She knew better than to try to climb it in its current state, but she plopped down on the bottommost step to pout.

"What are we going to do, Rí?"

I shrugged and stepped up to Bó to give her a nice pat down the neck. She stiffened a bit, her energy feeling much harder today than her usual wild, carefree spirit. It felt almost like … fear. Though I'd never felt that particular emotion from Bó before. I looked around to find a reason for it, but there was nothing out of the ordinary.

Just beyond her, the Killeen River gurgled softly. It ran under the castle and emerged here, at the old dried-up port. Long ago, a break in the curtain wall would have given access to the port, where the chieftains of old docked their boats. Now there was more than enough access, what with the curtain wall crumbling, but it didn't matter — there were no boats to speak of, no visitors, either, and the river had dried up to a tiny trickle long ago.

Even the land's natural defenses for the castle were falling apart. I just wished it didn't feel like we suddenly needed them. Desperately.

Because something called The Frenzy was inside me. And there seemed to be people in this world who wanted something from us.

"Moira's right, I think," Bríd said, and the admission startled me so much, I looked up. I hadn't noticed she'd moved to stand against the wall, one leg pulled up to rest against her other thigh, one eye closed. She opened them both now. "Nothing's okay. I think something's happened to Dad. Rí, do you think the pillow tells the truth?" She shook her head. "We wouldn't know, would we? All the things it's ever said, it's stuff from centuries ago. They could all be lies … right?"

At this kitchen table did Brian Doyle sign away his soul for those of his ruthless daughters.

I swallowed and avoided Bríd's gaze. Dad would do anything for us, that was certain. But who would he need to protect us from? As much as I wanted to believe the pillow was some gossip parlor trick with no veracity behind it … I didn't know what to believe anymore.

Bríd was deep in thought and didn't say anything else. Sighing, I laid my head against Bó's soft neck and ran my hand up her muzzle. She felt like velvet, and I slid my hand down over her cheek.

But something felt … wet. I drew my hand back.

My palm was covered in a crimson liquid.

Tearing myself away from Bó, I stepped around to face her head-on, looking for the injury. Great red drops were rolling down her cheeks, falling from her eyes. They left sticky red trails behind them.

Bó was crying.

Bó was crying tears of …

"Rí?"

My back was to Bríd, and I couldn't make myself move. She was by my side just a second later, her breath caught up in an audible gasp as Finbar flapped his wings, trying to regain his balance.

"Is that—?"

I could only stare at my hand, then at Bó, who closed her eyes for a long moment, then back at my hand. Bríd reached out and dabbed one of Bó's tears with her thumb. She and I stared at it for several seconds. Finbar gave a nervous squawk. Then Bríd brought her hand to her mouth and dabbed her thumb with her tongue.

Immediately, her face went scarlet. "Rí, go inside. *Abeg*, please." Her voice shook.

I shook my head furiously.

"Rí —" She turned to yell at me, but when she saw my face, she stopped short. The terror I felt was almost certainly written for all to see in my eyes and my mouth and my strangled breaths. Gulping, Bríd grabbed my hand.

"We can't tell anyone about this," she said, and her hand squeezing my own was shaking violently. "Especially Moira. Do you understand me?"

My eyes flew back to Bó. Was she sick? Why couldn't we tell anyone?

"Ríona!" Bríd snapped, shaking me. Finbar was dislodged from her shoulder, and he took to the air.

"Well, imagine meeting you here!"

We both spun around. It was Daniel Sheehan's apprentice. Louis. And he was stepping through the largest hole in the curtain wall, his hands in his pockets and an amused smile on his face.

Whether it was the blood on our hands or the terror in our eyes that tipped him off, his smile melted immediately.

"Are you all right?" he asked, hurrying his step.

That must have frightened Finbar, because he gave a loud screech and dove for Louis's head.

"Christ!" Louis dropped to the ground, throwing his arms over his head.

"Finny!" Bríd shouted, but I sort of hoped she'd let him chase Louis out of the yard. This was the last thing we needed a neighbor to witness.

"Why is there a bird attacking me?" Louis's confused question was muffled by his arms still atop his head, but Finbar was retreating. He gave one more threatening croak and landed on Bríd's shoulder.

Bríd stood in front of Bó, clearly hoping to block the real problem here, but even a slight Connemara pony is hard to hide. Especially one crying tears of blood. After Louis climbed to his feet, he went still.

His eyes going from Bó to us and back again, the shock on his face was absolute. But, strangely, he didn't say anything. I opened myself to feel something — anything — but I couldn't feel anything from him. There was some sort of wall around his person that kept him contained, not like other people. He only stared at Bó, his thoughts and feelings closed to me.

"She-She's sick," Bríd said desperately. But it didn't sound convincing. Finbar's caw of agreement made it sound even more hollow.

After a moment, Louis straightened and nodded, as if gathering his wits about him. "Should … Should I call Sheehan? He can—"

"No!" Bríd said quickly. "We, uh … We have a vet who looks after her." She clasped her hands and turned away from Louis, as if to dismiss him. "He's on his way, actually."

"Oh, I see," Louis said, nodding. He glanced at me, and I was caught staring at him openly. My palm was still outstretched in front of me, covered in blood. Louis cleared his throat and nodded once more before turning and hurrying back the way he'd come.

I was glad he'd left so quickly. But I couldn't shake an uneasy feeling. Why did it seem as though this wasn't the first time he had seen a horse cry tears of blood?

sáinnithe
TRAPPED

aidan

I was trapped. Stuck. Caught as a seal in a fisherman's net. I couldn't leave now, but I was too scared to stay. It was clear as the ocean to me now: These girls were far more involved in whatever was happening than I'd realized. And it was apparent they didn't know. The things I'd felt out there, the turmoil, the change that was happening … The girls were somehow involved. I just knew it.

And so I was terrified to stay. But I was also too terrified to go.

The newspaper shook in my fingers. My heart was beating too fast. I needed to calm down before somebody found me sitting here and asked why the Sunday paper had given me a mental breakdown.

I'd found it sitting outside the castle after hearing a thump against the front door and going to investigate. Moira was busy gathering up all the empty wine bottles upstairs and hadn't noticed the long minutes I stared at the tiny black-and-white date in the upper corner.

Nine and a half years.

Nine and a half *years*.

It had barely felt like a day.

Not that I felt the time passing out there. I'd existed apart from it. Beyond it. A place where there was no time, no place. Only need, and feeling, and water.

A smooth coolness slid over my skin, and for a moment I was back there. My lungs felt relaxed for the first time in days, my heartbeat slowing, as I existed and floated in the comfortable anonymity of the sea. But something didn't feel right. The animals around me ... they were frantic. My eyes snapped open.

The minute I'd stumbled out of the water that day, I'd felt it — time inching along, finally dragging me back into it. My brain struggling through the fog, desperate to emerge on the other side. And it had. It was swirled around every now and again, but I felt, largely, like myself again. My old self. Not a day older than I had been. But that was a farce.

Nine and a half years.

Rory would be a grown man by now. Did he have children? Was he still with Cora? Had they taken care of each other? Did they live in Ireland? Was he happy? Healthy?

Was he ... I mean, accidents happened. I knew better than most, people got sick, they ... I shook my head. Rory was still alive, wasn't he?

In the end, it was that last question that kept me at Bunrowan Castle. The longer I stayed there, the longer I could pretend my brother was out there, living a happy life but desperate to see me again. The longer I could prevent that last question from being answered, the longer I could guarantee my own happiness.

Because if something had happened to him while I was out there, I would never forgive myself.

anam marcáilte

A MARKED SOUL

louis

They'd clearly been caught unaware. As had I. That was the last thing I'd expected when I locked Conry up in my room at the Sheehans' and set out for their house with a story about stumbling upon the rustyback hill. I'd thought maybe I'd find them outside with their animals or doing chores. Maybe one of them would still be sleeping. I thought I'd find sisters going about their normal activities the day after their eighteenth birthday. Not *that*. I hadn't seen the omen for nearly a century.

In fact, for a split second, I hadn't understood what I was seeing. But the important question was: Did they?

The Morrigu seemed scared, but in a very human way. A visceral reaction to a terrible sight that she didn't understand. But the one called Bríd … Her terror was palpable. A living, breathing thing. I was fairly sure she knew exactly what the blood tears of a mare meant. And she

wasn't prepared to die.

Saving her would have been a pleasure. But her life meant little. She wasn't the one I was here for.

an t-arracht in ár measc

THE MONSTER AMONG US

bríd

The wind rushed through my wings, and I couldn't land, as much as I wanted to. Her body lay across the pebbles on the shore, but I wasn't in control. I couldn't reach it. And he stood there, at the water's edge, smoothing something in his hands.

Why won't you help her? I wanted to scream. But I couldn't. All that came out was a shrill crow's call: "Why? Why?"

As I watched, Aidan smoothed something in his hands and then pulled it over his shoulders like a jacket. He turned toward the sea, and the brown cloak spread over his body. He took a running leap and dove toward the water just as the strange cloak contracted and he transformed, in midair, into some kind of … animal. Without a backward glance at my sister, who lay dead on shore.

"No! No!" I shrieked.

But it was true.

I'd been right to question Aidan's ability to deal with that kelpie the day he'd saved my life. He'd known how to conquer it because he was just like it.

A monster.

Suddenly, I was staring into the dark. The dark of my room. And I was shaking.

Covering my eyes with my hand, I shook my head. It was a dream.

But I alone knew what had happened the very last time I'd dreamed someone else's death. There *was* such a thing as coincidence in this world … wasn't there? I'd had this same dream the night before, but I'd resolved to lie when Moira asked. If I continued to pretend I had only pleasant dreams for long enough, maybe she would stop asking altogether. That was the only way I'd stay sane.

A boom reverberated through my room. I looked around. Only a second later, there was another. It was coming from downstairs. Was that what had woken me?

Finbar cawed softly and swooped down to my shoulder as I climbed out of bed. The big mullioned windows of my room looked down on the bailey at the front of the castle, but I couldn't see anyone. If someone was at the front door, they'd be just out of my sight. But I did see something that made my stomach go cold.

The Whitethorn and Blackthorn trees that flanked the path to the front door lay ripped apart on the ground. They'd been butchered.

"M-Moira!" I yelled.

"Down here!" she responded immediately.

I ran down the stairwell and found her in Dad's room, pressed against one of the arrowslits that looked down on the front of the castle. She was white as a specter in her nightdress, her short red hair pulled high in a little knot. A few feet to her right was Ríona, peeking out the next arrowslit, Faolan up on his hind legs trying to get a look, too.

"Who is it?" I asked, rushing to join them. It was freezing in here, and I hadn't thought to bring my robe in my haste to get down here.

"Can't tell," Moira said. "But it sounds like—"

"Like they're trying to feckin' break in," I interrupted. Running to the small room in the corner, I wrenched open the old door and breathed in the must of centuries. The tiny chapel had no use to us now, so it mostly sat untouched. Kneeling in the center of the room, I tugged on the latch of the murder hole with all my strength. It groaned and lifted an inch. Peeking through it, I saw the front hall was empty, but as another boom rocked the castle, the front door shook, dust falling off it in a cloud.

I let the murder hole slam shut. We were in deep trouble. Someone — or some*thing* — had come for us. The kelpie. Or the old woman from last night. And I wasn't entirely sure Aidan didn't have something to do with it.

"It could be Dad!" Moira called hopefully. "He'd be confused why we blocked the doors. He could just be trying to —"

"There's something else," I said, standing and meeting her at the door to the chapel. "Something Dad wouldn't do." Moira stepped back and looked at me, concerned. "I saw the thorn trees from my window. They're all cut up."

Moira blanched. "What? Who would—?"

"What's going on?" It was Aidan, standing in the doorway of the room with one eye closed against the light of the moon filtering in through the arrowslits. His hair was a mess, and he was clearly still half-asleep. Unless it was an act. "Are you going to answer the door?"

"We have to do something," Moira breathed.

"*Now!*" Ríona signed.

"We could bar the door, j'know?"

"With what?" Moira yelled desperately.

I looked wildly around for something we could use. Castle doors were designed to open inward so you could secure them with a big wooden beam. We just didn't have any giant wooden beams lying around for that purpose.

The resounding smash that came from downstairs made us all turn toward the door. Not a single one of us had ever heard it before, but we all knew what it was. It was the sound of someone breaching the defenses of a medieval castle.

"Too late," Moira whispered.

"They're inside," I breathed.

Muffled voices and shouts — angry ones — came from downstairs, and even Aidan looked frightened.

"Did they just break in?" he asked softly.

"The murder hole!" Moira yelled, pushing past me.

"We don't have anything to throw!" I said, pulling her back. Besides, within seconds, they'd be past the murder hole, too.

"Then block the stairs!"

Ríona looked down at Faolan, and he sprinted to the door at once and took up position in the very middle of the stairwell, a tight growl in his throat and all the hair on his back standing on end. Then Ríona herself took off up the stairs, braids flying, and I heard soft thuds and scraping as she scoured her room for something.

Meanwhile, I scoured Dad's room for anything I could use as a weapon. But he kept things sparse. Besides a long, wooden table along one wall and his empty bed in the corner, there was nothing. Not even a shovel or poker for the fire.

"What do I do?" Aidan asked desperately as Moira grabbed a heavy hand mirror Dad kept hanging on the wall and took up position behind Faolan, wielding the mirror like a hurley.

I wiped a hand across my face. We were doomed. Moira hadn't played a sport since we'd been children.

"Just grab something!" Moira yelled. I needed to — and quick. This didn't match my dream, not at all, but I feared for Moira all the same. *This isn't how it ends, this isn't how it ends*, I repeated to myself.

It was as Finbar left my shoulder to perch on Moira's that I was struck with an idea.

One thing Dad *did* have in abundance was candles. Not by design. But the small room that had once been a chapel was littered with the debris of ancient worship, mostly dust, but also — candles.

"Matches! I need matches!" I yelled, running into the chapel.

"I know where those are — I'll get them!" Aidan shouted as I grabbed every stump of candle I could find.

As I reached the door with my bounty, Ríona met me in the stairwell with two things: the rifle that shot sweets, along with Faolan's blue silencing blanket.

Before I could ask how on Earth she was going to fight off attackers with a blanket, a voice reached us from down below:

"They're probably sleeping!" It was a deep voice with a thick Dublin accent. "Probably for the better!" A short chuckle followed that.

My heart beat faster. What did they want from us?

Aidan returned, tossing a box of matches at me, and I thrust the candles into his hands. "Here, hold these," I told him as I began lighting the wicks.

"What am I supposed to do with these?" Aidan yelped, eying the dangerously low wicks on quite a few of them.

"Nothing," I said, blowing out the match and tossing it on the floor. "Finny!" Finbar squawked and flew to Aidan's shoulder.

Aidan's eyes went round and he gulped as he watched Finbar out of the corner of his eye.

I didn't have time to comfort him. I turned to Ríona. "Is that all you could find?"

Shrugging, she tossed the rifle at me, and Aidan's eyes went even bigger. Unfurling the blanket, Ríona stepped up behind Moira and tensed. We were out of time.

"Morty, I smell something burn—"

The figure was no sooner around the corner than Faolan was at his knees, the stranger's leg clenched between sharp teeth, and Ríona was whipping him with the blanket.

"Ahh!" the man shouted before throwing a fist at Faolan. Ríona reared back with her own fist, but I yelled, *"Seachain!"* and she ducked. Faolan released the man's leg, and the guy looked up as I lifted the rifle.

"Bríd, don't!" Aidan screamed. I pulled the trigger.

A sweet shot out the end and hit the man in the forehead. It was taffy. Not the hardest of candies. But hard enough to hurt.

"Ow!" the man howled. I shot again. "They're shooting me, Morty!" the man screamed, stumbling down one step before catching his balance on the rope handle.

"What are you—?" A second man, Morty, pushed his partner forward from behind, and the guy faceplanted. Morty didn't have time to climb over his partner in the narrow stairwell. I trained my rifle on him. His eyes went wide just before a taffy pelted him in the eye.

"Ahhhh!" the man screamed, falling to his knees. Ríona dashed forward and dropped the blanket on the first man. She pulled the ends taut and waited as he struggled.

"What's going on?" he screamed, trying to free his arms. "What — Why is everybody silent? Morty, where'd you go? Why can't I hear anything?" The blanket had silenced the world, just as it did for Faolan every day.

"Finny, now!" I barked.

Finbar squawked in the affirmative and plucked one of the low-burning candles from Aidan's hand. He flew over the intruders and dropped it. The blanket lit at once, but Finbar was already flying back for another. Aidan watched in horror as the whole blanket went up and the man screamed. But his partner was right there stomping the fire out. Finbar dropped a candle on Morty, but he swatted it away and it went tumbling down the stairs.

"Get it off me!" the man howled, and Morty finally was able to yank the blanket off him. The movement sent them both tripping down several stairs, and I ran after them, my rifle trained on the nearest of them.

"What do you want from us?" Moira yelled from the step above me.

"Morty, let's get out of here!" The first man was flushed red, but he didn't appear to have suffered any burns. There was only a small gash on his leg from Faolan's attentions. His friend, however, had a black eye forming quite quickly. Still, he appeared ready to keep fighting.

I just wish I knew what for.

"Finny!" I yelled, and he appeared above me, a lit candle in his beak.

"Morty, *run!*" the first man yelled, and he was already halfway to the front door when his friend roared in frustration and took off after him.

I followed them all the way, only stopping on the doorstep, but Moira beat me there. She stood, panting, as Ríona and I caught up. The men were halfway through the bailey. Faolan ran as far as the mutilated thorn trees before stopping, barking once after our attackers, and then howling at the moon.

My limbs continued to shake as the men got farther and farther away. Finbar settled on my shoulder, and as he rubbed his beak against my cheek, I could feel it was warm from the candles.

"Jesus Christ," Aidan muttered behind us. Ríona stepped forward and took my shaking hand.

We watched until the retreating men disappeared into the dark down by the ocean. I watched a little longer to make sure they stayed gone. Then we both turned back toward the castle. They hadn't expected us to fight, I supposed.

Moira and Aidan embraced in the doorway, their intertwined

figures limned in moonlight. They pulled apart when they saw us, and Moira ran a hand over her face, a gesture that was likely half relief and half embarrassment.

My stomach twisted. I couldn't do this to my sister again. Break her heart. When had she fallen so thoroughly for this stranger without my noticing?

"What the hell was all that?" Aidan asked quietly, his voice shaking.

The look on his face — the wide eyes, the trembling lips, the pink in his cheeks — it infuriated me. I didn't know if it was being close to my sister or our brush with our attackers that made him look so frightened. But it didn't matter. He'd looked just like that in my dream as he'd walked away from my sister's dead body. It might break her heart now, but her life was more important.

I glared at him. "Why don't *you* tell *us*?"

deireadh leis na rúin
AN END TO THE SECRETS

aidan

"What are you talking about?" I looked between the sisters, every one of them shaken and exhausted. They each handled it differently. Moira looked relieved, Ríona near tears, and Bríd, well, enraged. They'd all valiantly fought off those men, defending their home and each other, while I'd stood useless, totally worthless, in every respect. But it hadn't been on purpose. Did Bríd think I'd been dead weight to give those men some kind of advantage?

That wasn't even close to the truth. But I couldn't deny that something weird had been going on. I could feel it, in the way the girls moved. The way Ríona seemed to know what people were going to do before they themselves did. The way Moira moved faster than anyone else. And Bríd … I didn't know what Bríd was thinking, but I knew it was bad news for me.

"You're keeping secrets from us," Bríd said, her bird swaying on

her shoulder as she jabbed a finger at me. "And it's time you came clean if you value your safety. Who were those men? What did they want with us? Why is someone trying to hurt us?"

"I have no idea!" I cried. I had a vague notion that these girls were intertwined in this land-deep reckoning the selkies felt coming, and a terrifying impression that the girls had powers I couldn't possibly understand. But I truly had no idea what was going on in this castle.

"I don't believe you," Bríd said plainly.

"Okay, we need to secure the entrances," Moira interrupted. "Now. You two can have your fight inside." She ushered us all back in the door. The wolf gave one last howl at the moon, then sprinted inside. "Ríona, will you find a chair big enough to barricade this door? I'm going to get Bó through the kitchen garden."

"You can't go alone," Bríd said quickly. "They're still feckin' out there!"

"I'll go," I said, desperate to be useful somehow, feeling pure relief at not having been kicked out into the night.

"No!" Bríd snarled at me. "You will march in front of me, in my line of sight, without making any sudden movements — wherever I go — until you tell us everything. D'jou hear?"

I stared at her. Could she truly know what I was? Was that her strange power?

Maybe it was time I told them everything. Hell, it had probably been time back when the kelpie had attacked.

"Well, let's do this quickly!" Moira chided. "*Oya!*" She led the way through the kitchen as Ríona hurried back down the hall lugging a large upholstered chair. It turned out the horse was as strange as the rest of them and was waiting in the kitchen garden, as if completely aware that her owner needed her.

Moira looked so relieved I thought she might burst into tears. Even Bríd looked relieved at the sight of the pony. She kept throwing glances at the creature, as if to check something. That Bó was still there? That she was okay? Moira ushered the small thing in through the kitchen door and down the hall toward the storage room where the magical hive was. Left alone in the kitchen, Bríd glared at me once again, her arms crossed over her chest.

"We should get that door locked," I said, nodding at the kitchen door behind her and avoiding her eyes.

She sighed, shaking her head, and went to do just that. It was a modern door with a normal doorknob, unlike the front one. She grabbed a kitchen chair and wielded it in front of her, making me jump out of her way. I firmly believed she'd do anything if she thought I was a threat to her sisters. She wedged the chair under the knob and headed for the stairs.

"Come," she shouted, and I ran after her, as obedient as her crow.

Her sisters were in the big living room, Ríona curled up around her wolf on the floor in front of the cold fireplace, and Moira standing at the windows. These windows looked down the back of the castle, but she seemed nervous, and keeping a lookout somewhere probably felt better than nowhere. If I'd learned anything by now, it was that she felt an intense and all-encompassing need to protect her sisters. I felt the urge to hug her, to comfort her somehow, but I knew if I so much as touched her now, her sister would suffocate me with the secret-whispering pillow.

Bríd stalked to the fireplace and turned on me. "Tell us. Everything."

"I … I don't know what—"

"Don't waste our time or insult our intelligence," Bríd snapped. "You're a monster. Aren't you?"

an selkie
THE SEKLIE

ríona

He didn't deny it. That was the worst part.

I didn't move to look at their faces. Because their thoughts and feelings were pelting me like we were in a huge festival crowd, and I couldn't wade out of it. Tears stung my eyes, and my mind struggled to clear. It left me exhausted, and I was still shaking from the fight.

"Aidan?" Moira said into the silence.

I squeezed Faolan tighter, trying to glean some calm, some composure from his steady breathing. He didn't move or try to wriggle away, and I was grateful for that. He seemed to finally be over his annoyance at being kept indoors at night, but he would be just as mad again when he realized his favorite blanket was nearly in ashes.

"Why won't you answer her, Aidan?"

Moira again. She still stood by the window, but I could hear it — feel it — all. It had been a long time since I'd felt her tender feelings

toward someone outside our family, but they were here now, and they were strangling me. Every second Aidan stayed silent, Moira's heartbeat grew louder, the whisper of a splintering heart deafening me.

"I should have told you earlier," Aidan said, defeat in his voice. "I'm more like that kelpie than I wanted to admit."

There was a soft gasp. "What does that mean?" Moira asked.

Bríd, for her part, didn't speak now. She wasn't enjoying what this was doing to Moira.

"I … I'm a selkie," Aidan said softly. "My real name is Fionn."

"You … " Moira scoffed. "You didn't even tell us your real name?"

Still, I didn't sit up. Their anger, sadness, fear, it was suffocating me, and I didn't know whose was whose. But I had no strength left for any of it. *This is worse than not knowing.*

Faolan raised his head and licked my cheek, erasing a few tears, and I hugged him tighter.

"What's a selkie?" Bríd asked, but her voice was calm now, controlled. For Moira's sake.

"Selkie," Finbar repeated. "Selkie."

I'd heard of them, of course. In storybooks. But Bríd didn't read the kinds of books I liked.

"We can transform into seals," Aidan explained.

There was a muffled moan, and I wondered if Moira was crying. I couldn't feel anything specific, just a tangled, gnarled mass of pain. *Make it stop*, I wished desperately.

Faolan pressed his soft forehead beneath my braids and against my neck, and I dug my fingers into his fur.

"And what are you doing here in Ballyconneely?" Bríd asked

evenly.

Aidan released a deep sigh. "Nine and a half years ago, I came here, to Ireland, to see my brother. That was when it all started. Well, that was when it all started again."

"So you are American? That wasn't a lie, too?"

There was a silence, and I knew that kind of comment from Moira cut Aidan deep. "I was born in the U.S., but my biological father was from Ireland. My mother … She was … from the sea." Aidan sighed again. "We were adopted when we were babies, and Mom and Dad — the ones who raised us — they didn't know what we were. They were just good, kind people who loved us. I don't even know … I don't know where they are now. How they are … "

"So how did you end up here on our hill?" Bríd asked. Her anger had receded some, and I was sure she no longer thought Aidan a threat. It let me relax a bit, at least enough that I could finally release Faolan and sit up.

The others stood in a stand-off, each in their own corner of the room. None of them even noticed me watching them now. Aidan looked crushed as he stared at the floor, as though his story was written there. "Rory and I only found out what we were the summer after I turned seventeen. The summer after I turned eighteen, I thought it'd be a good time to go back to the sea. That was more than nine years ago."

Bríd gaped at him. "But you're … "

"Still eighteen. Yeah, I know."

Bríd shut her mouth. Impossible things were happening around here all the time. A boy who could stay the same age for a decade was certainly a new one, but at this point, well, I could believe most things.

"I was sick for a long time as a child," Aidan explained, "and that summer after we learned what we were, I found out I'd relapsed. So I came here to Ireland, to Rory, to convince him to help me find what I needed to return to the sea and live as … as Fionn. That was my name before I was adopted."

"What did you need to find?" Bríd asked.

"My sealskin." Something passed over Bríd's face, but I didn't know what it meant. All I could feel was a tenuous, shaky thought like a thin string she'd just grasped but couldn't keep hold of.

"And you found it?" she asked.

Aidan nodded. "With our father. Our birth father. He was living on Inis Mór." That was just off the coast of Connemara.

"So you just left your life and went and lived out there?" Bríd asked, nodding toward the ocean.

Aidan shrugged. "I was scared of dying."

"Are you still … sick?" It was the first time Moira had spoken up. I couldn't feel anything but pain from her now.

He shrugged again. "I feel great. Even the kelpie wound is healing." He touched his stomach absentmindedly. "I feel better than I ever have before. Physically."

"Physically?" Bríd repeated.

"Well, I'm … worried. About a lot of things, but specifically, you three."

"Why?" Bríd asked — a little too quickly. Guilt poured off her in waves so heavy, I felt nauseous.

"The reason I came back," Aidan said. "There was a storm brewing out at sea. For a long time. The animals, they could tell something was happening. The land — Ireland — was changing. And things were becoming unsettled. I didn't feel safe there anymore. It wasn't something I consciously felt, but it was just there, in my bones. That's why I came back. To escape Ireland. To go home."

He looked around at each of us, his eyes falling on me last. His eyes looked as pained as his aura felt.

"Escape Ireland?" Moira asked helplessly. "What's changing?"

"I don't know," Aidan said, and this time when he said it, I think we all believed him.

At long last, Bríd cleared her throat and said, "I'm not sure it's such a good idea if you stay here any longer."

Moira looked at her, her eyes wide, but didn't say anything.

"Whether your story is true or not, the larger truth is that strange things have been happening since the day you showed up. That's a fact we can't ignore."

Aidan looked at her. "The day I 'showed up,' I saved your life."

"But how do I know you didn't endanger it in the first place?" Her voice was hard, but her eyes were on the ground and her energy was shaking. This wasn't the confident, surefire Bríd we were used to. This was a terrified one. "I just don't think I can trust you when you're … you're a … "

Aidan stared at her until it was clear she wouldn't finish the sentence. "If I'm a *monster*," he said quietly, evenly, "then so are you." His eyes were on Bríd, but they danced sideways to Moira.

"What?" Bríd snapped. "Because there're some cursed objects around this castle that we can't explain, or because we were kind enough to let you sleep in our feckin' house when we found you roaming around homeless and injured? Which one of those things make us monsters? Or is it something else, like?"

"You're keeping secrets, too!" Aidan yelled, taking a step toward her, the look in his eyes finally matching the frantic beat of his aura. "Locking yourselves up here, refusing to look at things for what they really are!"

"What the feck are you on about?" Bríd spat.

Aidan shook his head. "Have you ever stopped to think maybe it's not the curios that are magic — it's you?"

an t-ealú

THE ESCAPE

moira

The words didn't hit me like they did Bríd. She gaped, her mouth hanging open, but I merely turned to look out the window. I didn't begrudge Bríd her ire, but Aidan was right — she wasn't being truthful with herself. The curios were more than some "cursed objects" we found about the place. I'd known that since we were eight. When Dad had driven all night to get back from Dublin in time for our First Communion.

When he'd finally gotten home at six o'clock in the morning, he'd fallen asleep at the kitchen table. And then again while he'd been curling Bríd's hair with a hot iron. He'd nearly given himself a first-degree burn. In that moment, I'd wanted nothing more than for Dad to be able to stay awake long enough to be there for us, for my sisters, and when I'd gone to the pantry to find a snack for Ríona, who hadn't been able to eat for her nerves that morning, I'd discovered a fairy-sized

door beneath the bottom shelf. I'd never seen it before. Inside was a tiny plot of soil growing a mature coffee plant.

That was the very first time I realized the curios were sometimes, in a roundabout way, answering my deepest, most silent wishes. And then other things started to make sense. Like the tickling chair. In the weeks after Mam died, Ríona couldn't stand to see anyone sitting where our mother used to. She'd break down in tears and fly into a fury every time somebody did, even on accident. And then the tickling had started.

After realizing the connection between the curios and our wishes, I'd tried to manifest something specific when I needed it, but it never worked. It always felt outside my control — but only just. And now I couldn't help but wonder … were the curios somehow connected to what the pillow had said the other day? About Dad signing away his soul to protect us? Were they somehow a magic wrought from that deal?

"I don't understand it," Aidan said to the room at large, "but you're … you're all *different* somehow."

"Inhuman?" Bríd spat.

God, I didn't know she'd heard those whispers. That they'd called her that, too. It hurt me to know she'd felt what I'd felt in the face of that word.

"Yes," Aidan said, "and powerful."

"This is ridiculous!" Bríd shouted, and Finbar startled, taking to the air. Bríd huffed, working herself into a state. "We're not like you!"

"No," Aidan said quietly, "you're something more. I just don't know what."

Bríd deflated. "Why? Why do you think that?"

"Aside from all the magic? The levitating? The —"

"That's just the curios," Bríd whispered. "The mattress, the —"

"No." Aidan shook his head. "It's you. Why can't you believe that? Somebody else clearly does!"

"What do you mean?" Bríd asked.

"We have to leave," I said.

Everyone turned to stare at me. "Pardon?" Bríd asked just as Ríona signed, *"What?"* Only Aidan seemed to be in agreement. "Because this mad fella thinks we can do magic?" Bríd demanded.

"No, because we've been attacked three times now, by human and animal," I said. "Meanwhile, we have no idea where Dad is. We can't stay here."

Aidan nodded his agreement.

"Moira, we have nowhere to go," Bríd said.

"I might be able to help there," Aidan said shyly. "I need to find my family anyway. They might be able to help."

"Your brother?" Bríd asked.

"Well, we can start with my dad. If he's … still alive. He's … well, he's older."

"On Inis Mór?" Bríd asked. "That's not very far. Who's to say whoever's after us won't follow us there?"

"Well, they might. But he knows about, I mean, some of this stuff." Aidan shrugged. "It's a place to start."

"I don't know," Bríd said. She looked at Ríona, who looked just as unsure.

"Bríd, Ríona, we have to leave," I said again. "Whoever those people are who came here, they want something from us. And I don't want to wait around to figure out what that is."

"'Keep to the castle, and the castle will take care of you,'" Bríd quoted at me.

"But it hasn't, Brí," I said earnestly. "It's not taking care of us anymore. God, I don't know why. But it's not."

I held her gaze, and I could tell she knew it was the truth. Oh, how our roles had reversed. She'd been so eager to welcome Aidan into the castle and share all our secrets, but now, she wasn't ready to accept the implications. But I was. It was clear I could no longer keep my sisters safe here, so I had to find somewhere I could. It was in my veins, pumping through my heart, the need to protect us. But I couldn't do it alone.

"Please, Bríd," I whispered.

"I'm not leaving Finbar," she said quietly.

"Okay," I said. It would be difficult, but we could work with that. "I'll take Bó to Daniel Sheehan's, and Faolan … " I looked at Ríona, who was still curled around her wolfish baby. Her eyes were wet and glistening in the light from the fire. "He'll have to stay, too."

Ríona didn't meet my eyes, but she sniffed, and it made my heart ache. She wouldn't protest, not when so much was at stake. But it would break her heart to leave him. Just like it would break my heart to leave Bó.

"I'm sure Mr. Sheehan will watch over him, too," I assured Ríona, but I wasn't so sure. It would be easy enough to convince him to look after Bó, a normal pony who could get along with the few his family kept in their west field. But Faolan was a wolfish creature instantly feared by most who saw him.

Still, there was no other option. He couldn't come with us, drawing stares from every man, woman, and child who set eyes on him. There was no telling where our journey would take us. He wouldn't be allowed inside anywhere, so he'd be a hindrance. Finbar would be easy enough to hide, but Faolan …

At long last, Ríona nodded, almost imperceptibly, never taking her head from Faolan's fur.

"Okay," I said softly. "Then it's settled."

"I think we should wait until it's light out," Aidan said. "We want to leave without attracting attention, and so far, you've only been attacked at night. Well, by humans, anyway. If another kelpie comes after you in broad daylight on the ferry to the islands, I don't think you'll be able to avoid the attention."

"I agree," I said, all business.

Bríd only shrugged and caressed Finbar on the neck.

"There's something I need to get before I leave," Aidan said, clearly uncomfortable. "I hid it down by the shore. Will you come with me?" His warm gaze was on me.

"Of course," I said, my heart fluttering. The idea of being alone with him after his huge admission was intimidating, but I longed to ask him the thousand questions flitting through my mind. For some reason, for the first time in my life, they were things I didn't want to say in front of my sisters.

But Finbar squawked a warning, and Bríd stepped forward, her arms crossed. "She'll be going nowhere with you alone."

taobh istigh de mbrionglóidí
WITHIN DREAMS

bríd

"It's my sealskin," Aidan said, bowing his head. The sun glinted off his dark hair. "I can't lose it. I need it to, well, to transform."

Absently stroking Finbar, I tried to imagine Aidan as an animal, a creature, a spirit living beneath the sea, but it was no use. He was a boy, an American boy, about as awkward and thick and infuriating as any other.

Behind us, Ríona's anxious face was framed in the kitchen window. The doors to the castle were blocked up with chairs from the inside, and Faolan stood at her side, so I wasn't worried. I gave her a fortifying smile just before she disappeared from view as we went through the gate in the garden wall and emerged in the early-morning sun of the bailey.

Moira and Aidan walked ahead of me, talking softly, and though my heart felt I should give them some time alone, for Moira's sake,

there was no way my brain would go along with it. It was strange how our positions had shifted. Now I was the protective sister. I lagged behind, far enough to let them focus on each other, but close enough to intervene if I needed to.

And close enough to overhear their conversation, if I were being honest.

"Does it hurt?" Moira asked, her words hushed as she and Aidan squeezed through a hole in the outer wall. "When you transform?"

Aidan shrugged, and I rolled my eyes. What a chancer. Trying to play the big, strong lad. "Kind of," he said. "It's a bit … uncomfortable, you could say."

"You're so brave," Moira whispered, tucking a red curl behind her ear.

I yawned and scrambled after them, holding Finbar close to my stomach. He was knackered, dozing in my hand, his beak tickling my palm. We'd all slept little last night, and I was pretty sure Moira hadn't slept at all. Though, she was hiding it well now, behind those doe eyes she was putting on. I knew all about that, of course, and even fancied I'd taught her what little she knew. Still, I could see the bags beneath her eyes every time she glanced back at me and Finbar. While I'd sleepily gone through my things last night, looking for something that might be of use on this wild goose chase, I'd heard her moving around, opening and shutting drawers, in her room below mine. I'd tiptoed down and glimpsed her moving about in her room, antlers on her head. But I couldn't tell what she'd been packing. What things did Moira deem important enough to pack away for an adventure none of us wanted to be on? Once upon a time, I might have asked. But we were all on feckin' edge now.

"So what do I call you?" I heard Moira ask him.

He sighed. "As soon as I found out my birth name, I begged my brother to call me that. Fionn. I thought it was representative of who I should've been, had I been raised by my birth parents — an old Irishman and a selkie woman. I thought it was my 'real' name, and somehow I wasn't living my real life." He gave a bitter laugh. "Now, all I want is to be Aidan again. For things to be how they were before."

"Before," Moira mused. "So how long have you been eighteen?"

Aidan laughed — a real laugh this time. "I guess it's been more than nine years. Nearly ten. But I don't feel eighteen. I don't feel … anything."

"Well, you look eighteen," Moira said, and this time, her tacky flirting didn't make me want to roll my eyes. It hurt my heart. Because I had never seen my sister like this with a boy before, yet I couldn't forget what I'd seen in my dreams.

It wasn't the first time I'd had a dream like that. There had been a handful of times over the years that my dreams had coincidentally lined up with reality — the night I'd dreamed the school picnic was canceled for rain, the night I'd dreamed Dad would stay home rather than go to Dublin one weekend and we would spend the whole time playing rummy, the night I'd stayed up for New Year's and then dreamed I'd be sick in the morning from all that candy … They had all come to fruition. But there was only one other time that I'd dreamed of death.

I'd had nightmares before, of course. But they were always fleeting things that dissipated like smoke as I woke up. The night we'd turned six, however, I'd had a dream that had stayed with me like a memory when I woke, screaming.

I hadn't told anyone what I'd dreamed. Our mother, pregnant belly preceding her, had come rushing into our room. Back then, I'd shared with Ríona and Moira, when Ríona didn't crawl into Mam and Dad's bed in the middle of the night. That night, Mam had enveloped me in her arms, and I'd tried to get closer to her, to smell that calming scent of hers — coconut oil — and only feeling bitterness over the way the baby in her belly squeezed me farther from her. But almost immediately, I'd felt guilt — afraid that the only reason I felt that way toward my unborn sibling was because of what I'd seen in my dreams.

And everybody knew dreams weren't real.

That was what I'd been taught, anyway. And I'd never wished it to be true more than right then. Because in my dreams that night, I'd seen my mother, drenched in blood, cradling a baby in her lifeless arms.

That was the first secret I'd ever kept from my sisters. I hadn't told my mother, either. It wouldn't be nice to think someone's been dreaming of your death. And I loved her more than anyone and anything.

Of course, when Dad had come home from the hospital in Clifden one night, his face drawn, his hands shaking, I'd known what had happened before he spoke. And even then, I hadn't told anyone about the dream. Partly because I hadn't been able to see or breathe for the pain. And partly because I'd seen it as nothing but a coincidence, a sad, horrendous, horrifying coincidence, that my mother had died in childbirth when I'd dreamed just that.

"It's not here!"

The yell jolted me back to the rustyback hill, and I felt my hands shaking. Finbar's eyes were open, and he was looking steadily up at me. I had to get it together if I was going to be of any use when we left the castle. Moira and Aidan had gotten ahead of me, and Aidan was on his hands and knees beside a huge rock several yards from the beach.

"What?" Moira asked, bending down beside him to peek under the rock. Holding Finbar to my chest, I jogged to catch up.

"It's not here," Aidan repeated. "I hid it right here. Shoved it under the weight here, so the wind couldn't take it, and far enough away that the tide couldn't reach it."

He turned around, digging wildly through the grass around the rock.

"It's got to be here then," Moira said, so very helpfully.

Aidan froze and sat up, rocking back on his heels, his head in his hands. Was this desperation an act? If this thing was so very important to him, why hadn't he kept it with him?

"Somebody took it," he said softly.

"Nobody comes walking down this way," I said none-too-kindly. "It's too far from the village." If this was all a ploy, I was going to be feckin' furious. I just couldn't figure out what the point of it was, what this selkie boy stood to gain from it.

"Maybe it wasn't someone," Moira said. "Maybe it was some*thing*."

"Yeah, like a feckin' seagull," I snapped. "The poor eejit thinking he'd struck gold for dinner."

"I don't know," Aidan said, running a hand through his hair. He was the picture of despair. I just hoped it was genuine.

"If it was so important, why didn't you bring it with you?" I asked, trying to keep the suspicion out of my voice.

"I don't know," Aidan said. "Would you have welcomed a stranger wearing nothing but an old animal skin?"

"Well, we let you in knowing you were a thief, so —"

"It might be around here somewhere," Moira said, glaring at me. "Let's have a look around."

I shrugged and ambled aimlessly around, kicking at the grass, while Aidan and Moira scoured the place.

At long last, Moira stood and wiped her forehead. "Do you truly need it?" she asked Aidan bashfully. "I mean, do you intend … Will you … Will you go back? Back there?"

It was only then, as Moira motioned toward the waves, that I realized I'd seen this wretched thing in my dream. The sealskin. That was what Aidan had been holding as he'd watched Moira die on the shore. That was what he'd pulled around himself as he'd leapt into the water.

"Yes, he feckin' will," I muttered to myself. "When you need him most."

fán

STAY

ríona

They tried to leave me at home again, but there was no way I'd allow that. Not when they were taking Faolan away from me.

Aidan and Moira walked side by side on Bó's left, with Bríd tramping along on the pony's right. Fierce feelings of protectiveness were pouring off Bríd, and she kept petting Bó, as if she weren't trying to eavesdrop on Aidan and Moira and instead just wanted to be near the horse she had so very little attachment to. At least Moira didn't seem to notice. She was giving off a light, airy happiness, though it felt a bit forced. There was something more there, but I didn't even try to interpret it. I felt too weighed down by the feelings of suspicion rolling off Faolan as we trotted behind the others. He could sense something was wrong.

I was so wrapped up in my guilt that I didn't even notice we were no longer alone as we approached the Sheehan farm — until Louis was

only a few yards away, approaching Bó to give her a pat. It was unsettling, this emptiness I felt in the air around him. The lack of … well, anything. Like he could stop his emotions from touching me. Bó snorted a bit but was otherwise surprisingly open to the stranger's presence.

My eyes flew to Bríd. I'd been expecting to meet Mr. or Mrs. Sheehan, not their summer hand. Would Louis bring up what he'd seen in the bailey yesterday? What would Moira say when she found out what we'd kept from her? He was smiling big, his dark eyes glinting in the sun, as handsome as ever, but there was little room left in me to appreciate it. His dog was at his heels, and I felt Faolan bristle.

Leave it.

Faolan snorted but took a step back behind me. The other dog — Conry — for his part, was clearly not about to risk another meeting with Faolan, so he stayed put behind his boy.

"Well!" Louis said brightly. "What brings you all here?"

Bríd was already preening, fluffing her shiny hair in what I saw as a humorous imitation of Finbar. "We need a favor, actually," she said, stepping up in front of Bó and giving the horse a friendly pat. It was easy enough for her to be light and flirty — she wasn't parting with her best friend today. She had, however, left him at home for this little outing.

"Oh?" Louis said, his eyes taking in our little circus. "What might that be?"

"We're going away for a bit," Bríd said, crossing her arms airily. "We were hoping we could add a few souls to yer farm, j'know, till we get back."

Louis narrowed his eyes. "It's not the bird, is it?" he asked, looking around at the sky. "The bird hates me."

Bríd didn't seem worried Louis would give up our secret to Moira — her energy was light now, her worry over Aidan and Moira just a shadow beneath the glow she presented to the world. "Pshaw," she twittered. "He doesn't hate anyone. Regardless, he's not part of the package, I'm afraid. It's these two." She jabbed her thumb over her shoulder.

"Your sisters?" Louis said amiably, and his eyes were warm on my face. "We'd love to have Ríona and Moira to stay, but I will have to consult Mr. Sheehan to make sure. They won't mind sleeping in the barn, will they?"

"Very funny," Bríd said with a laugh as Moira rolled her eyes. Aidan was having considerably less of a reaction to this boy, which was very suspicious. He almost seemed to dull in Louis's presence, his double-sided aura going quieter. Though it was hard to shine in the presence of Louis's glowing gaze and bright smile and — Louis's eyes fell on me, and I felt my cheeks go warm.

"The pony and the dog," Bríd corrected him. "We were hoping to leave them with ye for a bit."

"Well, let me ask Conry, but I'm sure we can work something out." Louis kneeled and murmured, pretending to consult his dog, before standing again. "Yes, he says it's okay. But he does want to know where you're off to. And for how long."

"Oh, you know, off to see family in London, j'know? I was hoping for somewhere a little warmer, somewhere with a beach." Bríd winked. "But these dryshites insisted on familial duty and all that."

"How long will you be gone?" Louis asked again.

Moira piped up, glancing at Aidan. "To be determined."

"Ah." Louis looked at Moira for a long moment, and I fancied I could see thoughts flashing behind his eyes. But still, I felt … nothing. It was one of the first times I remember wanting to be able to feel someone's thoughts instead of wishing that strange part of me away. Louis finally seemed to gather himself and glanced at me quickly before settling back on Bríd. "I will say I'd rather hoped you all would be around. You know, to help this summer go a little quicker. The big Lúnasa party up in Clifden is only three days away."

"Oh, we'll miss that, unfortunately," Bríd simpered, as if we ever attended town festivals. "Not sure when we'll be back. But there'll be plenty of other birds there to entertain you, I'm sure."

"Ah. Well." Louis cleared his throat and glanced behind him. "I've, uh, got a lot to be getting to, so I'll go get Mr. Sheehan for you."

Without another word, he turned and walked off toward the house, whistling once to summon his dog.

Bríd stood there, looking gobsmacked at failing to keep the boy's attention. Moira glanced at Aidan, who shrugged. Only a second later, Mr. Sheehan came out of the house.

"What's all this?" he asked, a warm aura surrounding him like the glow from a fire, a good-natured smile on his face. "It's not every day we get a home visit from the Doyles, now, is it?"

Moira took over explaining things — at least our hastily made-up version of them — as Bríd had lost interest with the disappearance of the attractive young farmhand.

"And your da?" Mr. Sheehan asked when she was finished. "Will he be joining ye?"

"Yes," Bríd said, jumping in quickly. "He's actually still in Dublin. He'll be meeting us there."

"Grand, that's no problem at all," Mr. Sheehan said with a satisfied smile. Eying Aidan, his smile faltered. "Who might you be, lad?"

I didn't hear Aidan's answer, because Faolan was persistently nudging my palm. I kneeled beside him and rested my head against his. He whined, sensing that something unfamiliar was happening. I felt the same way. About everything. Everything that had happened since the day the kelpie had appeared.

It won't be for long, I promise.

Faolan nudged my cheek with his wet nose and let me touch the soft velvety fur there.

Mr. Sheehan kept asking Aidan pointed questions and didn't seem satisfied with the strange American's presence until Aidan had dutifully recited the counties in which each of his parents had grown up, where he'd grown up, and a number of other biographical facts. It was a half hour before Sheehan finally clapped him on the back with a smile. "Well, welcome home, lad." Then he turned to Moira.

"Now to the animals. Of course they're welcome here. Put the pony out in the field there, why don't ye? There's plenty there for him to enjoy."

"She," Moira corrected gently.

"Ah, of course. I do beg your pardon, madam," Mr. Sheehan said to Bó. "And here … " He went to the barn and returned with a lead. "You can use my Sadie's old lead to tie the dog up, so he doesn't try to follow you home."

My stomach flipped as he handed me the lead. I'd never put a lead on Faolan before.

My eyes flew to Moira. This wasn't going to work. What if Faolan went mad when we left? If not then, he'd certainly show his true nature when he found himself cooped up all night in a strange place. But Moira was already leading Bó away to pasture, Aidan following obediently behind her.

Swallowing, I took Faolan's head in my hands and pressed my forehead to his. *Don't hate me, okay? I promise it will be fine.* Before he could move away, I slipped the collar attached to the lead around his neck and fastened it. He whined a bit, stepping nervously around in my arms, trying to get a hold of the collar with his teeth.

Please. Believe me. Everything will be okay.

Faolan only whined louder.

Mr. Sheehan took the end of the lead from me, but I stayed at Faolan's side as he came to terms with being tied up.

I'll be back for you. Tears welled in my eyes.

I stood and took a few tentative steps away.

Faolan cocked his head at me and tried to take a step forward, but the lead prevented him. That only confused him more, and he tried to push forward again as I backed away.

Stop! Tears filled my eyes. Abeg, *don't do this to me. Stay.*

Faolan let out a desperate howl.

Please.

He stopped fighting and sat down on his haunches, his beautiful amber eyes big and round. I turned and ran as fast as I could.

I didn't stop until I was inside the bailey. Home.

Breathing heavily, I trudged through the archway into the kitchen garden. It didn't feel so much like home without Faolan bounding up to greet me.

Before I could think too much further on that, Finbar came soaring over the parapets, something big and white in his beak, and landed on my shoulder. I'd just barely opened my hands when he dropped a creamy envelope into them. Frowning, I flipped it over. It was addressed in an inky script:

My darling girls.

an litír

THE LETTER

moira

"I don't know." That was what he'd said. When I asked him if he was going back to the sea. Just *"I don't know."* God, it was absurd that such an answer was affecting me so much, but it was. That there would be a time when Aidan was no longer walking the Earth felt wrong and almost unbelievable. And the fact that I felt that way was categorically ridiculous. Bríd was up ahead, near the outer wall, her perfectly straight hair shiny and glimmering in the sun. Had it been her having such thoughts about a boy, I would have told her to come back down to Earth or get a grip or cop on already.

Which was exactly what I needed to do.

"I'm sorry you have to leave her behind," Aidan said, kicking at a pebble in the grass. He had his hands shoved in his pockets — well, the pockets of the pair of Dad's jeans he was wearing.

"It's okay," I said, suddenly feeling guilty. He'd assumed that was

why I'd been looking sulky, saying goodbye to my horse, but in truth, I hadn't been thinking of Bó at all. "It's for the best," I added weakly, hoping that made me sound kinder.

"Moira!"

Ríona and Bríd were standing in the archway to the kitchen garden, and Ríona was showing Bríd a piece of paper.

Aidan started jogging to catch up to them, and I followed, easily overtaking him. "What is it?" I asked.

Bríd only shoved the paper at me. Squinting against the bright light, I read,

> *My darling girls,*
>
> *I'm so sorry for the delay, and I'm so very sorry to have missed your birthday. We'll celebrate properly when I'm home. I'm missing you all, and I know you'll be worried. But please don't fret. All is fine, and I'll be home within a few days. I have only to get one more thing sorted. Expect me soon.*
>
> *Love,*
> *Dad*

That was just like Dad. A letter? A pen-and-paper *letter*? He was archaic to a fault. He also had a knack for poor timing. "God, why couldn't he have written a bit earlier?" I groaned, handing the letter over to Aidan. "*Before* we started losing our minds?" I looked up and met Ríona's shining eyes. She was ecstatic, and I saw the hope in her gaze. But I didn't feel the same. It would also be like Dad to write a letter to reassure us that everything was fine when absolutely nothing was, in fact, fine.

"What does it matter?" Bríd asked, Finbar on her shoulder. "The point is he has, and we don't need to go anywhere."

"He'll be home soon," Ríona signed.

"Yes." Bríd smiled. "We just need to be on the lookout until —"

"I still think we should go," Aidan interrupted, folding the letter back up.

Finbar cocked his head at him, and Bríd glared. "Excuse me?" she said quietly.

"I think we still need to go," Aidan repeated.

Uh-oh. Interrupting Bríd wasn't an activity most people lived to recount.

"Well, look who thinks he has the right to a feckin' opinion all the sudden!" she snapped.

Aidan's mouth popped open, but then just sort of closed again, like a fish. "He does," I said, glaring at her. "Because without him the other night, who knows where we'd be now?"

"You serious, Moira?" Bríd laughed. "He was completely feckin' worthless when we were attacked. He's about as useful in a fight as an actual seal."

"Worthless! Worthless!" Finbar squawked.

"That's fair enough," Aidan said, "but seals are actually quite viciou—"

"And what about the kelpie?" I said, interrupting him, my eyes shooting daggers at Bríd. I didn't mean to, but I was seething. "You were handling that so well on your own, were you?" I shook my head. "We'll make these decisions together, or not at all."

"All right." Bríd crossed her arms. "I'll go with not at all."

I rolled my eyes. Typical Queen Bríd drama. "What?"

"I'm not going anywhere, like," Bríd said. "So you can go ahead and make your little decisions and leave without me, if that's what suits."

"What are you talking about?" I demanded.

"Look, he only wants to go to find his family," Bríd said, nodding at Aidan, "and you only want to go to please him. But this isn't a game, and whatever's been going on here needs to be known to Dad. If he comes home to an empty castle, imagine what he'll think."

She wasn't wrong, but the thought of staying here, like a bunch of sitting ducks, was scary, too. And, perhaps more importantly, I didn't appreciate what she'd said out loud about me wanting to please Aidan. How would he take that? The embarrassment was what made me take the low road.

"And this has absolutely nothing to do with that lad flirting so shamelessly and going on about parties and the pair of ye" — I nodded at Ríona — "mooning over him, hmm?"

"Yeah, Moira, that's it," Bríd said darkly. "Because I'm so desperate for a boy's attention that it's all I can think about right now. Oh wait, no, I'm not as hard up as you."

Bríd grabbed the letter from Aidan, who stood speechless behind me, and turned back to the castle, Finbar taking to the air above her. "You'll have to go without me — because I'm not leaving."

Ríona hesitated a moment before following.

cosaint amhain eile
ONE MORE DEFENSE

bríd

Finbar and I were sitting beside the stove in the kitchen when Ríona came downstairs. It was warmer upstairs in the living room, of course, but being cooped up in a room with those other two was more than I could handle right now. Moira, back to those feckin' antlers, clutching lamely at some feeling of control, and Aidan, so obedient, so considerate … while simultaneously deftly manipulating my sister. I didn't know what they'd decided regarding my ultimatum — though you could be sure they'd be deciding it *together* — but they hadn't, as far as I knew, left yet.

"They still here?" I asked as Ríona pulled a raggedy old upholstered chair closer to the stove and plopped down.

She nodded and gave me a small smile. At least one of my sisters was in agreement with me: we had to wait here for Dad. I glanced down at the letter again. Every time I did, my thoughts went a little

fuzzy, and I couldn't think straight. I supposed I was tired. Regardless, what I knew for sure was that despite Dad's reassurances in the letter, something had obviously gone wrong on his trip. I wanted to know what — and if it had anything to do with what was going on here at home.

But I was more scared than I'd let on that Moira might call my bluff and decide to go off with Aidan anyway. It wasn't that I didn't trust Aidan, it was just that … Well, I'd seen what I'd seen in my dreams, and so I suppose I didn't feckin' trust Aidan.

And he clearly wanted to go find his family. Our dad's letter was a slight hiccup in that plan, so if he wheedled Moira even the tiniest bit, I was pretty sure she would run off with him. And then what?

I would go with them, that was what. She wasn't going to be left in that creature's clutches, that was for sure.

Across from me, Ríona had a heavy old-fashioned oil lamp in her lap. It was rusty and cumbersome, but, to my confusion, it was flashing, flaming one moment, extinguished the next.

"What's it do?" I asked.

"Do, do, do," Finbar squawked. I hadn't seen the lamp before, but if Ríona was lugging it around, there was a good chance it was another curio turned up unexpectedly.

Ríona shrugged and held it up as if to say, *This.*

It continued to flash as Ríona fiddled with the top and took off the handle and then put it back on and just generally messed around with it.

"And Aidan thinks this is *our* doing?" I scoffed, nodding at the lamp. "Like *this* is what we'd create if we could perform some sort of magic."

Ríona shrugged, her eyes downcast. *"Maybe,"* she signed.

Immediately, I felt guilty. I knew Ríona felt more for the curios than I'd ever understand, but it was just ridiculous to think this dumb flashing oil lamp or my levitating mattress or the tiny plant that grew money was our doing. We didn't even know how they *worked*. And not a single one of us would be wasting a power like that on creating a dictionary that sang rebel tunes, that was for sure. Whatever it was that created the curios, it was something far more random — and boring — than any of us.

The lamp flashed uselessly at me in Ríona's lap. Sighing, I started a game of fetch with Finbar. After I flicked a piece of lint across the room, Finbar would go soaring after it, only to return a moment later with something completely different — and usually shiny. I'd collected two buttons, a decorative spoon, a thin twig, a hairpin, a tiny screw, and an earring I'd lost ages ago, and was thinking of going up to see what those other two had decided about my ultimatum, when Ríona kicked me.

I looked up.

She was holding the lamp with one hand and pointing out the window with the other.

And sure enough, there was someone in the kitchen garden.

I jumped up and was about to yell for Moira and run for the sweets rifle when I saw the dog. A big, lanky dog that looked an awful lot like a wolf. My eyes darted to the person. It was Louis.

"What's he doing here?" I mumbled. Ríona shrugged, but her smile was huge and her hopeful eyes were only for her Faolan. I went to the kitchen door and pulled it open. "Are ya trying to scare the shite out of us?" I called.

Louis laughed good-naturedly. "Ah, you lot are still here, then? Tell me, why would a friendly visit from a neighbor scare the shite out of you?"

"There's just been some weird things going on around here, that's all," I said, gesturing for him to come in. "Welcome to our gaff." Faolan bounded in ahead of him, his tongue lolling out. He was usually very good about waiting to have his paws wiped clean by Ríona, but he was obviously too elated to think of manners at the moment — and so was Ríona. She was on her knees, her arms around Faolan's broad neck as he slathered her face in slobbery dog kisses.

"Arah, that's gross, Rí," I grumbled.

Finbar hopped out from under the kitchen table, looking perplexed, a single pearl in his beak. He dropped it as Louis stepped inside, and I closed the door behind him. Finbar squawked in warning and flew at Louis, but I intercepted him deftly and tucked him to my side, careful not to ruffle his feathers. Louis looked alarmed but clearly wouldn't admit it.

"That was his way of saying *hello*," I lied. In truth, I had no idea why Finbar had reacted to him that way. We were all clearly too on edge these days.

"The welcome to this place is certainly one-of-a-kind." Louis laughed. He looked around the room, and I watched his reactions carefully. It wasn't every day we had a stranger in the castle. Though, we had, to be sure, recently admitted another. But I still wondered what it looked like through Louis's eyes. Our life.

"So," I said, trying to distract myself, "we ask you to watch Rí's dog, and you thought you'd just send him back to an empty house, like?"

Louis laughed again. "Actually, this one has a mind of his own." He jabbed a finger at Faolan. "He got the best of me back at Sheehan's and acted like he'd just escaped a high-security prison. He ran straight for home. I ran after him, of course, but I just barely caught up with him here."

Louis wasn't breathing heavily or anything, and he'd been ambling pretty comfortably in the garden, so I wasn't sure about the veracity of the claim that he'd *run* after the escaped dog, but it was no difference to me if Faolan had a nice jaunt around the countryside by himself. After all, that was what he did *every* night. Louis just didn't know that.

"So are you all not leaving today?" Louis asked.

"We're not leaving at all," I said, more confidently than I felt.

"Oh?" He raised his eyebrows, anticipating more information, but there was none I could give him that wouldn't just make things sound even more deranged.

Tentatively loosening my grip on Finbar, I waited to see if he'd go after Louis again. A croak escaped his throat, but it was the resigned kind. I let him stand up on my palm and lifted him to my shoulder before going back to my seat by the stove. "I'd invite you to sit," I said to Louis, gesturing to Ríona's vacated chair, "but you must be so energized from that sprint across Ballyconneely."

Louis glanced at Ríona, who was still on the floor with Faolan. The beast was rolled over on his back for a belly rub. "To be honest, I'm exhausted. I would love a kip by the fire."

"If you fall asleep," I warned, "Finny here *will* take the opportunity, j'know?"

"Know, know," Finbar repeated.

"To what?" Louis demanded, heading for the chair across from me. The flashing oil lamp was sitting on the floor beside Ríona, and Louis glanced at it as he stepped around it, but he didn't question it. For a moment, I wished he *would* ask about the lamp, because I'd probably tell him. I didn't know if it was jealousy of the way Moira had taken to Aidan, or just disappointment that the very first person to learn our secrets had featured in my nightmares in a way I couldn't ignore, but either way, the result was that I wanted to tell someone else. The secrets, the fears, the fight we were in the middle of. And Louis seemed as good a person as any. He was here, anyway. Which, admittedly, wasn't the highest of standards, but when you lived in a creepy old castle with your strange sisters, people who didn't run in the other direction were already one thousand percent better than most.

"Come now," Louis said, and his accent had never sounded posher. "Don't keep me in suspense. What does your bird dream of doing to me?"

I smiled. "There's truly no telling," I told him honestly.

Faolan gave a soft howl as Ríona had stopped petting him. Rolling her eyes, she lay down on the threadbare carpet in front of the stove, and Faolan followed her, collapsing on her knees. She went back to scratching his belly in the warm glow emanating from the tiny square window in the stove front. I saw Louis watch it all with a small smile, and then his eyes wandered back to the flashing oil lamp.

"So." Louis sighed, stretching his legs out toward the stove and crossing them at the ankles. I liked to see him feeling so at home here. It made me feel like maybe we weren't so very strange after all. "Tell me, then. What strange things have been going on around here that have you all scared of the neighbors?"

I looked at Ríona; she looked at me. Feeling like we weren't so very strange had been a very brief daydream.

Holding my gaze, Ríona signed, *"No."*

But Moira was still upstairs with the selkie, oblivious to what was going on down here. We could've been dragged off by a kelpie with opposable thumbs by now, and she would be none the wiser. All because she was wrapped up in Aidan. And I'd been the one to make the case for bringing him into our confidence in the first place.

Yes, my first attempt at creating a confidant had clearly failed. I didn't feel any safer or more understood with Aidan knowing our secrets. In fact, I felt like we needed even more protection.

And maybe, if Louis was on our side, too, Moira would feel more comfortable staying here at the castle. You know, with more backup. Or maybe she would just be too scared to leave us alone with him if he knew our secrets. Either way, the result was the same: it would keep her here with us until Dad got home.

At long last, I looked back at Louis. "Do you promise not to tell? We haven't gone to the guards, and we're not going to."

His smile faltered. "My lips are sealed."

"Someone … burglarized … the castle. Last night, while we were here." I chose my words carefully, as I wasn't sure just how much to tell him yet. An attack would be highly suspicious, but a burglary, that was fairly standard, wasn't it? Not around these parts, but maybe where

Louis was from.

He stared at me, his eyes evaluating. He didn't look shocked so much as … curious. He looked at Ríona. Then back at me. "And why won't you go to the guards?"

Ríona's head snapped to me.

"We have our reasons," I said haughtily, hoping my tone would be enough to keep him from asking more.

It wasn't. "But if you're in danger … "

"We can handle it," I said. "We think." Louis raised one thick eyebrow. "Well, we are here alone until our dad comes back," I explained, "and we're not rightly sure when that will be. A few days at most. But until then, well, we feel a little vulnerable out here alone. Vulnerable to … to burglaries, obviously."

"As you would be." Louis smiled gently. "Well, I would be honored to help you ladies however I can."

"Really?" I asked, taken aback. A boy like Brian Brennan would have had a thousand and one questions to ask before ever promising anything so gallant.

"Really?" Finbar repeated.

"Of course," Louis said.

I smiled gratefully. "Well, would you mind … just being here with us whenever possible? Just to help protect the castle and everything. In case, you know, the thieves come back. There's no telling what they were after."

"To protect the castle. Yes, of course. Must protect the castle." He was teasing me, but I didn't mind. "Of course I'll stay with you all."

Ríona's gaze was prickling my neck, but I knew what it said —

Moira's not going to like this. "Just in case those feckers come back," I said again, more for her benefit than his. Her gaze turned away from me, but I was pretty sure she was shaking her head.

Louis smiled and glanced at Ríona. "I would be honored."

"To what, pray tell?" Moira stood in the doorway of the kitchen, her hands on her hips, antlers tucked under her arm. Aidan stood a few steps behind her. How she found the righteousness to stand there like that looking at us chatting away in the kitchen when she'd been upstairs *alone* with a boy was beyond me.

Louis stood, like some kind of old-timey gentleman, and nodded at Moira. "To defend your honor!" He pantomimed wielding a sword.

Moira looked alarmed. "My what?"

Just what had she been doing upstairs with Aidan after all? I wondered.

"To help defend the castle," Louis said, more seriously. "In case those predators come back."

"Who exactly are you talking about?" Moira asked, her eyes flying to me. She knew, of course, and she was silently reprimanding me for telling him. But I didn't care. She and Aidan had probably come down here to announce they were leaving. Would this stop them? "And what exactly are you doing here?"

"The cheek on you, Moira!" I snapped. "You could be a little less rude to a guest. Especially one who was graciously watching our animals for us. Is that how you return favors?"

Moira crossed her arms over the antlers pressed gingerly against her chest. "I don't see Bó anywhere."

"Faolan ran away, and I only just caught up with him here," Louis explained. "I'll bring your horse back tomorrow since you're not leaving. But I do think it's best if I stick around tonight. I agree with Bríd; those thieves are likely to be back. I'm sure they think the castle is brimming with antiques they can sell somewhere for an easy fortune."

Moira was positively glaring at me now. "Oh, you heard about that, did you?" she said through clenched teeth.

"You have quite a little army forming," Louis said, his eyes on Aidan.

"Army?" I laughed. "You haven't seen that one in a fight."

"Are you serious, Brí?" Moira yelled. Finbar huffed up, unsettled. "God, I can't believe you right now!" Apparently, I'd hit a nerve. "Why did you tell him?"

"I'm sorry. That's what we're doing now, *abi*?" I asked, gesturing at Aidan. "Isn't it? Telling random strangers all our secrets."

"Uh," Aidan mumbled, "I think—"

"Oh, that's rich, coming from the person who told Aidan everything in the first place!" Moira said, interrupting her beloved. "What's caused this sudden change of heart? It couldn't be the boy who just stumbled into the village who doesn't know anything about you and thus doesn't know to avoid you, hmm?"

My stomach dropped.

It was one thing to hurl insults at each other that we only half-meant. But I knew Moira meant this one from the bottom of her heart. Her face said it. As well as her tone.

"Well, what did you decide?" I said calmly. "Isn't that what you've been up there discussing? Are you off or what?"

Moira narrowed her eyes at me. "You haven't answered my

question. Why did you tell *him*, of all people?" She pointed at Louis, who was being impressively calm at the moment, despite having just walked into a house occupied by a family who was clearly altogether deranged. "A random stranger?"

"I told him so that he'd stay here with us so that *you'd* feel safe enough to stay!"

Moira just stared at me for a long moment. Finally, she rolled her eyes and shook her head. "Right. You did it for *me*. I'm sure that's what was going through your mind. As if you've ever, one single day in your life, ever thought of somebody else before doing something mad."

"You—"

A slam interrupted us.

We all whirled toward the kitchen door.

Ríona stood there, Finbar on her shoulder, Faolan at her side, a tiny angry pack who could only speak through the slamming of a door. But speak, they did.

Ríona shook her head and stalked to the middle of the room. Finbar stayed put on her shoulder, which told me he was quite angry with me. It could've been for the forgotten game of fetch as much as for the yelling. Ríona pointed from me to the chair I'd vacated, and then from Moira to the hallway leading to the stairs.

It had been a long time since we'd had a mother to punish us, but we understood the concept. We were being put in time-out.

Moira growled in annoyance and stomped out of the room, while I plopped down in my chair, pretending to feel triumphant. I hoped my face was reflecting that farce because on the inside, I felt broken. Moira and I fought all the time. But why did it feel different this time, when we had an audience? Almost as though, if she said those things to me in private, I could chalk it up to normal sister fighting. But if she yelled them in front of relative strangers, she truly meant them.

I was losing my sister to a boy. That much was clear. But that was the best-case scenario. Isn't that what happened to sisters as they grew up? The circle of life and all that. No, that wasn't the reason I felt short-tempered with Moira and my heart beat so fast when we fought. I knew the real reason, even if I couldn't admit it to anyone out loud.

I was losing Moira every night in my dreams. And the longer I ignored that, the more likely it became that I would lose her in reality.

an fairtheoir

THE SENTINEL

moira

"I'm sorry," I said, setting a steaming cup of tea down on the stone. "I just can't leave without them."

"I know, and I wouldn't ask you to," Aidan said. He was leaning against the crenellated parapet, his forearms dotted with goosebumps as the bats darted and danced in the light of the moon above him, giving off a squeaky little chorus. Aidan's eyes roved the darkness beyond what little light the castle threw over the rustyback, but I couldn't see anything out there, and I wondered if he could, or if he was just doing it out of habit. Maybe what Bríd had said about him being useless had cut a little, after all. I mean, I knew what it was to feel a fierce need to protect what you loved. Not that I imagined he felt that way about us or anything, but … Well, he watched the dark as studiously as if he could fend off any possible attackers that way.

"I brought you tea," I said. "I wasn't sure if you drank tea over in

America or … you know, out there." I laughed a little as I awkwardly gestured toward the ocean at our backs. He gave me a stiff smile. "But the girls were making some, and it tends to get cold up here at night, so I thought I'd bring you some. It's the go-to Irish cure for anything. Even a gash like the one you've got." I nodded at his stomach.

"It's healing," he said, looking away, not even glancing at the tea. After an awkward moment, he muttered, "Is he still here?"

"Um, yeah. They're down in the kitchen, drawing up battle plans like we're in some sort of proper war. Ríona's showing him all the trap doors and things. He's quite interested in it all, actually."

"I don't trust him," Aidan said, shaking his head.

A quiet laugh escaped me, and I tapped my finger against my lip. "Hmm, why does that sound like something *Bríd* would say about *you*?"

"I mean it," he said, and for the first time, he stepped back from the parapet and looked at me. "What was he doing showing up here tonight, when he knew we were leaving? Why was he poking around what he thought was an empty house?"

"W-Well," I stuttered, "Faolan ran away —"

"Right. Very convenient."

A bat landed on the stone beside Aidan's hand, and he pulled back with a hiss. The tiny thing squeaked at us, and I reached out to pet his soft, furry head. Aidan gulped and watched it take flight again. It was easy to forget that, as wild as the things he'd told us were, there were parts of our life that were still strange to him.

"So … what?" I asked carefully. "You think Louis was turning up here to rob us or something? That stuff he said about thieves wanting to ransack the castle, you think that's what he was going to do? Surely he's heard from Sheehan by now that there's nothing to ransack here."

"No," Aidan said softly. "That's not what I think."

"Well, what is it, then? He's a stranger, so I'll give you the risk of stranger danger, that's true, but beyond that … I don't think he's much of anything."

Aidan sighed and looked up. The bats were squeaking furiously above our heads. "I don't know."

"Well, we've been robbed before," I said slowly with a soft smile. Aidan looked at me sharply, clearly concerned. "By you." I nudged him with my elbow. "God, Aidan, don't you remember being caught red-handed trying to make off with our washing?"

Aidan didn't crack a smile. "I don't think he was here for your dad's clothes."

"Then, what do you think?"

"I think … that letter from your dad wasn't real."

I stared at him. "What?"

"Did you notice the letter arrived right after you dropped the animals at the farm and he found out you'd be leaving? That's a weird coincidence, isn't it?"

"Aidan," I said, shaking my head. "Why, pray tell, would he forge a letter trying to get us to stay here if he wanted to rob the place? He'd want it empty. It doesn't make a lick of sense."

"I don't know," Aidan said, hanging his head. "But maybe … "

I waited. "Maybe what?"

"Maybe he didn't want the place empty. If it wasn't the castle's treasures he was after. If he was somehow in league with those men who attacked … "

I nearly laughed out loud. He was so set on making Louis some sort of diabolical villain when there was absolutely no evidence that he was anything but a boy who liked the attention from my sisters. He wasn't the first of those, and he most likely wouldn't be the last.

But then again, I understood the assurance that could come from naming your enemy. Maybe this was all getting to Aidan more than I'd known and he needed a visible enemy to conquer. Because the alternative — that we had no idea what was going on — was far scarier. That much I agreed with. But the rest …

"It's written in Dad's handwriting," I said gently.

"Is it?" Aidan raised his eyebrows.

I frowned. "Well, I'd have to look at it again. I wasn't really scrutinizing it. But … Aidan, if it were a forgery meant to make us sitting ducks, then why wouldn't Louis have attacked us when he arrived here tonight? When everything would have gone according to his plan — if that were indeed his plan. It just doesn't make sense."

Aidan sighed. "I know. But something just doesn't feel right."

Smiling gently, I rested a hand on Aidan's arm. "That's true enough. But I don't think it's for the same reasons you think."

"I wouldn't be so sure of that," he muttered.

"Aidan?" I said after a moment. I took a step closer to him. For some reason, I needed to be nearer to him to have the courage to get the words out.

"Yeah?" he asked, glancing at me. When he saw I'd moved closer, he straightened. Then took a step closer to me.

That was all the courage I needed.

"Do you really think we're somehow involved in the curios? And the things they can do?"

He looked down at me, and even in the chilly darkness, his gaze filled me with warmth. He grabbed my hand and threaded his fingers through mine. "Yes."

I looked away, blinking rapidly. My eyes were suddenly a tad too full of water.

"Why don't you believe it?" he asked. "Have you ever … tried? To make one? Or … do something else? Make something happen?"

I gulped, suddenly disagreeing with my earlier decision — it would've been a lot easier to have this conversation if I weren't standing so close to him. "Yes," I breathed.

He slipped one hand around my neck, brushing my hair away from my face with his thumb. "And?"

I shook my head, just barely, afraid any movement would break me out of this spell, pull me out of his arms. "I can't control it. Not overtly. But … " I sighed as his thumb came very close to my lips. "God, sometimes it feels like the castle is … listening to my wishes. Which is mental, I know. Absolutely insane."

"It's not." Aidan took one step forward, closing the distance between us. "If my existence can teach you anything, it should be that nothing is insane."

His lips were electric. Even on my tiptoes, I wasn't tall enough, but he bent ever so slightly, pressing his lips against mine. He was warm and sweet and even the spots where his hands rested on me felt electrified. When he pulled away just a moment later, the chilly air rushed in between us, and I wanted nothing more than to banish it again. But the shock of my first kiss was too much. Pressing my hand against his where it still rested on my neck, I giggled.

He looked alarmed at first, then smiled, too.

"You know," I said, "I haven't exactly seen any proof that you really are what you say you are. How do I know for sure? It's not like I've ever seen you in action, out there." I nodded vaguely toward the ocean.

His smile died down, and a little crease appeared between his eyes. "Would you like to?"

My own grin melted away, my heart beginning to hammer in my chest. The idea terrified me, and I wasn't sure I wanted to see — to truly know — that it was real. And I wasn't sure I'd be able to believe my own eyes if I did. But, most of all, the thought of seeing him out there made him seem so far away that it made my stomach turn. Finally, I admitted, "I don't know."

We heard laughter from downstairs, and Aidan sighed loudly, dropping his arms back down to his sides. "I'd feel a lot better about all this if *he* weren't still here."

"Aidan," I said gently, rubbing his arm. "Don't worry. Louis doesn't know what's going on any more than we do."

I'd never been more wrong in my life.

geall

A PROMISE

ríona

The night was my time. When all the world was asleep, and no one's thoughts bombarded me but my own. And, tonight, my thoughts were on Bríd.

She was curled around the secrets pillow, too far gone to be bothered by its whispering now. After we'd shown Louis all the castle's ancient defenses — which he'd found endlessly fascinating — we'd moved upstairs to the living room. Moira and Aidan had never appeared, though shortly after one, I'd crept upstairs floor by floor and found Finbar asleep in his roost, Moira fast asleep in her bed, and Aidan standing like a sentinel before the parapet, staring out at the sea and completely unaware of the bats flitting about his head.

I'd come back to the fire and found Faolan asleep while Bríd eagerly entertained Louis with stories of old inhabitants of the castle. Secrets we'd gleaned from the pillow. Though she didn't tell him that.

Not yet. He was eager and interested, but, for once, I was forced to learn that not from emotions made visible to me, but from his actions. Like the fact that he was always smiling. He had the kind of smile that made your own grow without your realizing it. Even if I couldn't feel anything from him, not like I could others, he made his emotions clear enough. I found myself listening to the stories I'd heard a thousand times and enjoying the theatrics from Bríd that normally grated. And even though most people would have left me to sit quietly by myself, Louis brought me into the conversation at every opportunity with an "Isn't that funny, Ríona?" and "Ríona, do you believe that?" And it didn't bother him that my answers were always silent. I'd laughed, my cheeks warm from the fire, until the others had fallen asleep.

But now my attention was on Bríd. I could see it, even as she slept. The loneliness.

I thought briefly of what Moira would say if I told her Bríd was lonely. She'd never believe it, because she saw only how the boys fawned over Bríd and how Bríd pranced through the world on a crash course for adventure. But I understood. Bríd felt alone in the world in a way that Moira never would. And I thought it was getting all the stronger now that Moira was drifting away from us to be with Aidan. Though, I knew that wasn't the root cause. I knew that because this feeling, this sense of loneliness, was always there in Bríd. So much so, I hardly noticed it anymore. It was a soft, murky thing that hung around Bríd's shoulders like a blanket — something to give an approximation of warmth in the worldly absence of it.

And it was, I realized, a feeling I'd seen before. The memory came back to me so quickly I felt dizzy. It was our mother, walking slowly down the path away from the castle. Bríd, Moira and I stood at the door, whining and crying and generally being awful. Mam tried to hush us before she left, but we wouldn't hear it. And so she gave Dad a weak smile and pulled that murky shadow around her and held it tight like a shawl and set off to catch the first of the three buses it would take to get her to the nearest salon that could braid her hair.

Loneliness wasn't quite the word. But I didn't have a word for it. I picked a long curl off my shoulder and slid my finger up the coarse ringlet. Whatever it was, I could feel it within me.

Faolan whimpered at the window, jarring me back to the castle. He was up on his hind legs, his front paws on the windowsill just beside the picture of Mam. He'd been relatively calm all night, considering I'd kept him inside again, but as the faint glow of sunrise spread over the castle grounds outside the window, he pressed his nose to the window and whined again.

What is it? I asked him. He only whimpered louder.

I disentangled myself from the old blanket I'd wrapped myself up in during the night and climbed off the sofa. I hissed in a breath as my feet touched freezing-cold stone. Careful not to knock against the couch Louis was sprawled across — a much less attentive protector than Aidan, to be honest — I tiptoed quickly to the window and put a hand on Faolan's back. His hackles were raised, and he whined low in his throat.

You need to hush up, Faolan. I scratched his head quickly, trying to placate him, but he wouldn't be calmed. Frowning, I looked down at the sea and over the foggy fields above it, then across the trickling river, draped in mist, and into the bailey …

There, on the outer bailey wall, stood a dark figure.

My body went cold.

The sun had only just begun to break over the east side of the castle, so the bailey was cast in shadow, and everything was cloudy with the haze of a Connemara morning. I couldn't make out who was standing on the crumbling wall, but they wore a brown leather duster unlike anything a Ballyconneely resident would be caught dead in. Faolan gave a sharp bark.

There was a noise behind me, and both Faolan and I whipped around. He dropped into his defensive crouch.

But it was only Moira standing in the doorway.

I breathed deeply, my hand on my chest, and Faolan gave an annoyed *ruff*.

"You kept him in again last night?" Moira asked, watching Faolan as she stepped into the room, hugging herself against the chilly air. "What are you looking at?"

Breathing heavily, I turned back to the window. The figure had climbed off the wall and was leisurely strolling away into the mist. I bit my lip. Aidan was set on leaving here, and Moira was determined to make him happy. I couldn't give her a reason to leave. Not now, when Dad was on his way back to us. Something was going on, and only Dad could make it right. In the meantime, I would make sure the doors were barred at all times and somehow convince my sisters to stay indoors.

Finally, I shook my head and gave a little shrug. The figure had disappeared completely in the morning mist.

Faolan gave an angry snort and stalked over to the fire. I followed him, avoiding Moira's eyes. She watched me for a moment, her lips set in a firm line, but then her eyes landed on Louis.

"Arah, it's time to get up!" she yelled suddenly.

Louis started, as did I, and Bríd shot upright, her hair as tangled as Finbar's nest. "Wass happen?" she babbled.

Moira sighed heavily. "Everyone's getting up for the day," she said, marching to stand behind the couch Louis was sitting up on, rubbing his eyes.

"Getting up?" Bríd repeated, squinting at the window. "It's barely sunrise."

I felt uneasy being reminded of the time. Why had someone been standing outside our house before sunrise? Rubbing the gooseflesh away from my arms, I stood again and went back to the window. There wasn't a soul to be seen, but for the seagulls riding the wind down to the water.

Faolan harrumphed. Everyone ignored him, including me.

"Yes," Moira said sternly. "If Dad gets home and sees a stranger has slept the night on our couch, he won't be thrilled."

I rolled my eyes. Since when had Aidan ceased being a stranger? Luckily, Bríd was still half-asleep and incapable of putting together that argument.

Yawning big, Louis stood and stretched. I glanced over my shoulder at him. His shirt lifted as he raised his arms toward the ceiling, revealing a thin strip of skin. "Ah, yeah, I should be going," he said, smiling at Moira. "Glad to see everyone's made it through the night in one piece." Then he turned that smile on me. "Goodness, Ríona, how long have you been up? You look as refreshed as if you'd slept the day away."

I grinned and gave a little shrug. I felt like I hadn't slept a wink, so he was certainly having me on now.

"Yes, yes, she's the picture of health," Moira grumbled. "Come on with you."

"Don't be such a cow, Moira," Bríd said, but it held no vitriol because her eyes were closed, her cheek had fallen against the couch cushions again, and she was already half-asleep. I turned back to the window. The mist was beginning to dissipate, leaving the familiar sights as clear and green as ever. It felt silly to imagine someone watching us now, on the wall that had been there all our lives, in the bailey we'd played in since we were toddling. But I knew what I'd seen. And so did Faolan.

"Thank you for staying with us," Moira said curtly, marching Louis toward the door.

"Of course." He tipped an invisible hat at her, and then sidestepped her, like a sheep escaping a sheepdog. "Ríona," he said, stepping quickly to join me at the window. He knew he was on borrowed time. "I just wanted to say … " He reached out and touched my arm.

Faolan gave a grumble from beside the fire but didn't move.

Louis's touch was warm, his fingers soft. I looked up at him, wondering what on Earth he could have to say to me. "I don't want you worrying. Everything is going to be fine."

Something pricked behind my eyes. Was the worry, the fear, that apparent on my face? Or could he just read me like no one else could? Moira certainly hadn't noticed, and Brí was dead to the world.

Still in shock, I forced myself to nod, a stiff, shaky movement that certainly disclosed how Louis's being so near affected me.

He smiled. "I'll be back tonight, if you'd like?"

His hand fell away from my arm, but the spot stayed warm, burning with the most delicious feeling, as if that single spot on my skin would never be cold again. I nodded.

His smile broke open. "Good. I'll see you tonight."

With that, he turned and let Moira shepherd him out of the castle like a good little guard dog. My real guard dog only glared at me.

ar an dé deireadh
ON BORROWED TIME

louis

A thief. That was what Bríd said had attacked them. In a way, she wasn't wrong. But that depended on how you defined the term *thief*. And I wasn't going to be so generous as to pretend that was all this was. Either way, I couldn't discern how much the sisters knew, but if attackers were already upon them, they would need to know soon, or hand their lives over in ignorance.

Of course, that explained the omen. If word was out already, then the sisters had very little time to figure out how to protect themselves, and that meant I had very little time, too. The hordes would descend soon enough. Though I had little idea what form they would take. Regardless, the omen seemed to indicate the one called Bríd would die at their hands.

No matter what, I had to act soon.

It was a shame, really, that Medb couldn't have gone about this

another way. But things were already in motion. That didn't mean I couldn't improvise a little. Since I'd be going back to the castle anyway, as I'd promised The Morrigu, maybe I could save her sister's life while I was there.

misneach

COURAGE

moira

I'm not sure what finally convinced me to gather my courage, go down to the kitchen and get out the letter from Dad. But I did. When the others weren't around. I didn't want Aidan to know his theories had gotten to me, and I didn't want Bríd or Ríona to know I was so paranoid.

I laid the letter on the table and smoothed it out with my palm. Leaning over it, I gazed at every word. My mind went fuzzy, and I rubbed my eyes. What was I looking for? My head throbbed. Maybe the drama of yesterday had gotten to me more than I thought. Perching on the nearest chair, I squinted at the way he wrote his name. *Dad.* My eyes crossed, and I felt even more confused. Could Aidan be right? Could someone have forged this letter?

Dad.

I shook my head. This was utterly ridiculous. Why was I standing here scrutinizing every letter? Neither of my sisters had noticed anything strange, and neither had I until Aidan started spouting his theories. No. This was Dad's handwriting.

Shaking my head, I folded the letter up and replaced it in the drawer where Bríd had left it last. I was losing it. We all were. Our grip on reality. We had to get out of here.

Why couldn't Bríd and Ríona see that?

cumhacht

POWER

bríd

We were on full high security, per Moira's terms of staying and waiting for Dad. The doors were barred, the pony, retrieved from Sheehan's, was inside, the murder hole was open and beside it was stacked planks of wood. Ríona and I had taken to climbing in and out of the kitchen window to avoid the trouble of unbarring the kitchen door, but even that had been outlawed by Moira. We were all captives.

Faolan tilted his head upward and gave a loud, trembling howl at the ceiling of Ríona's room. Ríona only glared at him. He snorted and gave a sharp bark. Honestly, being in the middle of these two was almost as bad as being the third wheel with Moira and Aidan.

Even Finbar had no time for me. He stood in the opening to one of the corner bartizans, an overhanging corner turret adorned with holes for shooting arrows through. Of course, it had been some years since the bartizans had seen anything through those holes but the bats

that Finbar watched curiously now. I could hear them squeaking, and it sent chills down my spine.

"I don't know how you can stand it up here," I grumbled, talking to no one in particular. "Living with bats."

There was exactly zero response.

Groaning, I fell backward on Ríona's bed.

My head connected with something hard. "Feck!" I grabbed the base of my skull and cursed the pain away. Ríona studiously ignored me. Various curios covered her bed, not to mention the floor, the old escritoire pushed up against the wall, and the window wells.

She sat cross-legged at the foot of her bed, staring intently at a small slice of soda bread sitting on a plate atop the velvet quilt she'd had since she was a baby.

"What are you doing?" I asked for about the third time.

For the third time, she ignored me.

She closed her eyes for a long moment and when she opened them, she was positively glaring at the bread.

Groaning yet again, I stood and walked over to the window. Finbar hopped a little closer to the bartizan, and the bats' screeching grew louder.

You're not captive, I wanted to shout at them. *Get out of here!*

Outside, the sun wasn't yet set, just growing weaker, the light watered down a bit, like every summer evening. The light would linger late, never fully giving up, until the sun rose again. But it was no use to me when I couldn't be out there enjoying it. A current hummed through my veins like usual, begging to be let out. I briefly considered flaunting Moira's rules and going to run wild around the rustyback. But we were already on thin enough ice as it was. No, the empty fields around the castle would have to stay empty. Even Bó was down in the lower chamber with a good deal of hay.

Here we were, all locked up like Troy, anxiously awaiting a giant wooden horse any moment now, and nothing was happening. Except our sitting around, refusing to live our lives until Dad came home. Which was worse than nothing, in my opinion. If I'd known how very strict Moira would become, I may have let her run off with Aidan.

Something moved down in the bailey. I squinted. "Rí, we have a guest!"

Ríona looked up, alarmed.

"It's Louis," I said, rolling my eyes at her fear and heading for the door. Even if everyone in this room hadn't been ignoring me, Louis would have been a welcome distraction. "Are you coming?"

"I'll be down in a minute," she signed. But she had that same frustrated look on her face she often had when I interrupted her reading. Shrugging, I skipped downstairs, past the door to the storage room, which was temporarily Bó's barn, where Moira and Aidan murmured to each other now. They hardly had a word for anyone else, save Bó. I felt indignation rise in me and didn't even try to beat it down. I'd be able to push this weird envy away once Louis filled the castle with his laughter.

Downstairs, he was already climbing through the kitchen window.

"You should really lock that," he said with a smile.

"Shh!" I snapped. "Don't let Moira know I unlocked it!"

Finbar swooped into the room then, finally curious about where I'd gone. But when he landed on my shoulder and set eyes on Louis, he just gave an annoyed squawk and flew off again.

"Someone's in a mood today," I said, flopping down in a chair by the stove. "Actually, a lot of someones in this place."

"Oh really?" Louis sat in the chair beside me. As he did, his sleeve pulled up, revealing a tattoo on his forearm.

"What's that? I asked.

"Oh, a tattoo," he said casually, pulling his sleeve down.

"I know that, like," I said with a smile, reaching to push his sleeve back up. His skin was warm beneath my fingertips, egging me on. I traced a finger over the three-sided spiral.

"It's a triskele," he said. "Just an old Irish symbol."

"What's it mean?"

There was a clunk, and we both jumped, turning just in time to see a plate of freshly baked soda bread appear in midair and clatter onto the kitchen table alongside a butter knife.

We both stared.

Not another living soul moved in the room.

My heart hammered, making it difficult to breathe.

"Was … Was that always there?" Louis asked, his voice a bit strangled.

"Yes?" I said.

But the look on his face told me he didn't buy it. And looking into his warm eyes, I suddenly didn't care. I'd told him about the attack, and he'd become a chivalrous protector. What would happen if I told him about the curios? Moira had told her beau, and look where it had gotten us.

Locked up in the same old castle we'd been locked up in for years.

"Actually, no," I said.

Louis raised his eyebrows.

"Strange things happen around here all the time," I said, and everything in me stilled, waiting, unable to draw breath. "Things we can't explain. Things that seem … magical, j'know?"

He looked at me. Truly looked at me. And it felt like the first time I'd been seen all day.

"Like what?"

I hesitated only a moment.

The little potted money plant was sitting on the windowsill, shoved aside since we'd been using the window as a door. Ríona had kept the little plant in her room for a while before realizing it wouldn't grow much without full sun. I presented it to Louis, palm stretched outward.

He inspected it. "Not quite what I was expecting," he murmured.

"Look." I nudged the coin growing in the dirt near the little plant's base, looking up just in time to see Louis's eyes go wide.

"You don't mean it's *growing* that?"

I nodded, placed the plant in his palm, and went to the table. I dragged the tickling chair over to where he stood. "Sit."

He laughed. "Why?"

"Just do it, like."

He did, and the familiar reaction came over his face — a mix of mirth and astonishment — just before he leapt out of the chair. "How is it doing that?" he yelled, his face flushed.

Going to the kitchen counter, I grabbed the old biro and a piece of paper and handed them to Louis. "Write a lie. Go ahead. Try to."

As he set pen to paper, I opened the stove and grabbed the

everlasting match from its spot at the edge of the fire. He laughed softly as he wrote. I looked over his shoulder as the words *Louis is the one true God* rearranged into *Louis is a base servant* on the paper. A weird way to phrase "farmhand," but more or less true, I supposed.

"How does it do that?" he breathed.

Without replying, I held out the match. He took it eagerly. "What does it do?" he asked, staring at it.

"Blow it out."

He did. Or tried to, anyway. The flame flickered and lengthened, burning a deeper orange.

Louis licked his fingers and pressed them together over the flame. The flame burned bigger. He took it to the stone fireplace and stepped on it. Smashed his shoe across it. The flame burned on. Laughing, Louis took it to the kitchen sink and let water run over it. The flame burned brighter.

"Louis, the whole place is full of stuff like this," I said, holding my arms out at the castle around me. "We don't know why."

"This is incredible," he said, laughing out loud as he dashed back to his chair. The match in one hand, he picked up the potted plant again and touched a finger to the shiny coin. "This is … This is unreal!" And he babbled a bunch of other things that fell away from my ears as I watched his face.

He was intrigued, of course, just like he'd been with the murder hole and the oubliette yesterday. But that seemed to be the extent of it. He didn't think we were freaks, some otherworldly witches better left at arm's length — or halfway across the countryside. No, he just seemed … interested.

And that made his smile all the more endearing.

"There's something else," I said, and he broke off in the middle of whatever he'd been saying.

"Something I've never told anyone before."

His brows pushed together and he leaned forward.

"I can predict the future. Sort of. Sometimes." I shook my head and dropped my face in my palms.

"What do you mean?"

"Jaysus," I groaned, tears stinging my eyes. Why was this so hard to put into words? This thing that happened to me so many nights of my life, why couldn't I talk about it? "I just … I have these dreams. And they have sometimes turned out to be true."

Louis was looking at me like I was a curio, too.

"Can you tell my future?" he asked.

"No," I said quickly. "I can't just *do* it, j'know? Just make it happen. I'll just have a dream and then it'll repeat again and again every night until I want to tear my hair out, until … until, well, it comes true." I paused. "And sometimes they're about death."

He looked at me strangely then. Through the tears I couldn't stop, I tried desperately to read his reaction. There was pity there, certainly, but interest, too. And … it almost looked like he was worried for me.

Leaning forward, I grabbed his hand. "Tell me I'm not feckin' mad, Louis," I breathed.

"You're not," he said softly.

And those were the sweetest words I'd heard in a long time. Squeezing his hand, I bent forward.

The apprehension appeared in his eyes like a cloud moving in on a summer day. He stood. "I-I should go," he said, already three steps toward the door.

I sighed. It wasn't the first time I'd scared a boy off by moving too fast. They'd flirt till the cows came home, but the moment you made a move, they were scared little boys again.

Suddenly, he stopped. Paused. Turned.

"A-Are your sisters around?"

I nodded. "Upstairs."

"Ah, I was just, just thinking about the Lúnasa party." Twiddling his thumbs awkwardly, he stepped toward the hall. "I'm just going to nip up there and see if they want to go."

And he scurried away, joining the ranks of people in this castle who were getting on my last nerve.

cuairt tráthúil

A TIMELY VISIT

louis

The grass was dewy as I walked back to Sheehan's. I didn't stay the night at the castle. My thoughts were too jumbled for me to properly keep up any sort of facade, and even though my time was running out, I couldn't do it. No, it was a better idea to retreat and sort my thoughts out before returning tomorrow for the final bombardment.

When you sacrifice them for good, a little voice in my head hissed.

Closing my eyes, I pushed a hand through my hair. Never had those girls seemed more like lonely little clueless children. It was all down to Bríd. I'd been thoroughly amused when she'd wanted to share her secrets with me — that she believed in magic. But those enchanted objects were more sophisticated than they should have been. They were clear products of specific needs, wants. And the dreams? If what Bríd said about her dreams coming true wasn't an exaggeration, she was having visions. That meant these girls were far more powerful than

Medb or any of the others would be expecting.

And that could be a problem.

But that wasn't what made my hands shake now as I pressed them into my pockets.

Tomorrow was Lúnasa. And I couldn't get Bríd's tears out of my mind.

They were helpless. Clueless. Distraught. And I was now one hundred percent positive they knew absolutely nothing of what they were, why I was here, or what was coming.

And they didn't deserve it.

So what if I couldn't do it? What if I couldn't go through with it?

I absently ran a finger over the triskele on my forearm.

The front door to the Sheehans' modest farmhouse was unlocked as usual. But today, Conry didn't come bounding around from the back of the house to greet me. That was unusual. Maybe Sheehan had brought him inside since it was so late. I crept quietly up the stairs to the guest room, but my hand shook on the knob so badly, it rattled. Not wanting to wake anyone up, I let go at once. Taking a deep breath, I willed myself to calm. This kind of powerlessness was the last thing I needed the night before I had to act.

If I acted at all. What if I bailed instead?

I could do it. Run away now. Tonight. Get on the first boat to mainland Europe. Make my way east and stay there, far away, for as long was necessary.

Opening the door, I slipped inside the bedroom. How would I sustain myself? I hardly had the money to get out of Ireland. Could I get far enough away that she couldn't reach me?

I flipped on the lamp atop the bedside table.

A man was sitting in the chair beside it.

I jumped three steps backward but managed not to scream.

The man stared at me, his hairy face devoid of emotion. "You're certainly out late, laddie," he growled. He wore a long brown leather coat and heavy black boots. Mud covered more of him than not.

I swallowed, willing my voice to stay even. "Who are you?"

"Medb sent me," he said simply.

My heart beat faster. "Why?"

"Seems ya aren't performin' as well as'd been hoped. There's some questions as to yer abilities. What's takin' so long 'xactly?"

"Th-They just turned eighteen," I stammered, fighting for control of my voice. "They were of no use until then."

"Ah, but that weren't part of the plan, hmm?" The man shook his head with a smile, baring a set of brown-stained teeth. "I s'pose 'er Majesty thought ya should've had 'em well in hand by then." The man chuckled, but it sounded more like a humorless cough. "Now, laddie, myself, I thought ya had 'er that day outside with the horse, I mean, ya had a mighty look goin' that day, ya did, with the hair and the smile and all, but then the omen, nobody coulda predicted that now, to be fair."

My heart stopped. "Have you been watching me?"

He barked out a horrible coughing laugh. I glanced at the door but didn't hear any footsteps. Maybe Sheehan and his wife really would sleep through this.

"Would ya align yerself with the Queen of Connacht and not expect some accountability, would ya?" He snorted. "No, laddie, Medb wants to be remindin' ya of 'xactly what your job here is.

"I know what my job is." I gulped. "Tomorrow is Lúnasa. Medb knows that is when I am at my strongest."

He laughed again, and this time he had to wipe tears from his filthy eyes. "Ah, ya. The sacred time. I've heard you lot did that. Waitin' around to get yer power from somewhere else. Not strong enough to just do it yerself. S'pose that's why yer where ya are now, innit?"

Anger pulsed through me, but the man was twice my size. Not to mention he was the one with Medb's full trust. I obviously hadn't earned that. "Well, it worked for us for thousands of years," I said quietly.

"Until it didn't." Medb's henchman climbed to his feet. "Best be thinkin' up something clever now, laddie. Wouldn' want ya failin' on me." He clapped me on the shoulder, but it was meant to intimidate. And it did. It hurt like hell.

Then he opened the door and strolled out into the hall, not a care in the world. "By the way," he added, pausing at the top of the old farmhouse's stairs. "I had to lock yer beast up in the barn. You'll want to be teachin' tha' one some manners, you will."

As the front door slammed shut behind him, the truth hit me like a bolt of lightning. I couldn't run away. Not now. Not ever.

I might've been a god, but Medb wielded the wrath of a once great queen feeling her last chance at power slip away. There was nothing more dangerous than that.

an file

THE POET

ríona

The oil lamp flashed one, two, three times. I sighed and rubbed my eyes. I still had no idea what the lamp's function was, but I was too tired to suss it out now. I'd stayed awake half the night with the secrets pillow pressed to my ear, trying to glean some further information about Dad. But all I heard were the same old secrets — or lies — of chieftains and gentry from long ago. That had been my last-ditch effort at being proactive after spending the day trying to make a curio. Aidan's theory that we controlled them was too tantalizing to ignore, and I'd thought maybe that was what The Frenzy was. It felt to me like the curios were always in answer to a specific need of ours. So I skipped all my meals yesterday until I was starving, and then sat up in my room staring at a slice of soda bread, willing it to get bigger or multiply or become a big delicious loaf of bread or do *something*. I stared at that soda bread for over two hours. To zero effect.

Yawning, I scooted closer to the stove and closed my eyes against the flashing of the lamp.

Faolan's sharp bark startled me awake just as a door creaked.

I jumped as the old kitchen window swung open.

Louis. Of course. The only person I could never feel coming.

"Why, hello," he said, climbing down from the kitchen sink and closing the window behind him. The lamp flashed brighter and brighter and I shoved it under my chair. Faolan snuffled around Louis's boots briefly and then returned to his spot by the stove. He was used to Louis by now and let him hang around without too much fuss … as long as Louis's dog, Conry, wasn't around.

"How are you doing this fine Lúnasa evening?" Louis asked brightly as he took a seat across from me.

Honestly, he was the only boy I knew who cared a wit about the ancient Celtic festival, but it was kind of endearing. With a weak smile, I gave him a shrug.

"That great, huh?" Louis asked, shaking his head. "I suppose we'll have to change that."

My smile grew a bit.

"So, uh … " Louis looked at his hands in an uncharacteristically awkward move and then glanced around the kitchen. "Where is everyone?"

I shrugged and pointed upward, twirling my finger. *Around the place.* Bríd was most likely still holed up in her room like she had been most of the day, and Aidan and Moira were probably keeping Bó company, but neither had been confirmed.

"Good." Louis smiled, a warm, sweet smile that reached right through me. "I was hoping to share something with you."

Faolan raised his head to stare at Louis. I raised my eyebrows.

"I … well, I write poetry sometimes," Louis said with a self-deprecating laugh. "And I was hoping you'd read some." He leaned forward and pulled a folded-up piece of blue paper out of his pocket. "You … Well, Ríona, you sort of seem like the only person who would understand." His fingers looked impossibly strong and handsome as he held the little square of paper out to me.

My cheeks felt hot, and my heart began to beat a little faster. I felt a little out of control of my hand as it reached out to take the paper from him. Was this what it was like to fall in love? My hands shook as I unfolded the paper, and I felt vaguely nauseous. Why did Bríd like this? Why did people write books and songs about this? Taking a deep breath, I read.

Golden, quaking, crisp
the Earth goes searching
for a promise once made

And I meet a golden girl
in a castle by the sea

The pact is still strong
the harvest restored
the people fed another year
And there lives a golden girl
in a castle by the sea

The solstice gone,

the equinox in approach

but the world stands still

For me and a golden girl

in a castle by the sea

When I glanced up, my eyes felt like pools of water, but Louis was staring at me, his brow furrowed, and I had to look away immediately. How could such a handsome human care so much what I thought of his words? Worrying about other people's opinions was for the likes of strange girls who lived in secluded run-down castles on the edge of the world. You know — freaks.

Inhuman freaks.

That was what a boy had called me once.

But now I knew what another boy had called me. *A golden girl in a castle by the sea.*

I swallowed. Faolan nudged my foot, but I didn't look at him. If I did, I would cry.

"That bad, huh?" Louis raised his palms to his face and shook his head.

My smile was uncontrollable. It was halfway between a grin and sob, and it took all my concentration to keep it steadily unreadable. Carefully setting the poem down on the hearth next to me, I jumped up and grabbed a clean sheet of paper and the truth pen from the kitchen table. It had spent the last two years or so untouched on the kitchen counter, so I'd wondered over the fact that somebody had moved it.

But I hadn't yet had a chance to ask my sisters why they'd needed to test somebody's honesty. Still, it would do for my purposes now. Because I had no intention of lying to Louis.

Sitting back down across from him, I perched the piece of paper on my knee and carefully wrote,

It's beautiful.

As he read the words, the worry disappeared from his face. But he still said, "You really think so?"

Louis didn't know it, but this pen wouldn't let the user write lies. I couldn't tell him that of course, so, instead, I wrote,

Really.

I nodded enthusiastically, ignoring Faolan's grumpy snort, and Louis grinned. "Well," he said, and the grin was pushed away by a strange sadness in his eyes, "I was Ollamh Érenn once upon a time."

What's that? I wrote.

He smiled rather sadly and shook his head. "Just an old title … a, um, an award … in school." It was strange being with someone whose thoughts and emotions I couldn't see. I didn't think he was telling the whole truth, but I couldn't *see* it. Couldn't *feel* it. The experience was strange and … thrilling. He cleared his throat and stood. "Do you want to go for a walk with me?"

I forced a weak grin and bit my lip, turning back to the paper. *It's too dangerous. And Moira would have a fit.*

He nodded quickly. "Yes, of course."

But there's another way we can be outside.

He looked at me expectantly, and I stood, making sure to bring the paper and pen. I never wanted to stop talking with Louis. Going to the door to the hall, I nodded for him to follow me. Faolan jumped up, but I shook my head.

Stay here. Just this once. Please?

He stopped and cocked his head at me, and I looked away quickly, before I felt guilty. Glancing once more at Louis, I took in the handsome smile on his face, a close-toothed grin that made me feel excited and comfortable all at once. Smiling, I turned to lead the way.

Maybe this falling-in-love thing wasn't as bad as I'd thought it would be.

lúnasa
LÚNASA

ríona

It was windy up on the parapets, but barely colder than the castle. I pulled my sweater tighter around me and leaned against the west corner, pulling my thick mass of curls back over one shoulder, but it sprung free immediately. Down below me, the bats would be stirring in the bartizans, ready to take to the skies for the night. I wondered what Louis would think if I showed him their little home in the corner of my room. He'd probably think I was a monster.

Tucking a loose ringlet behind my ear, I glanced at him. He stood with his hands in his pockets, one arm resting against the old stone of a parapet as he gazed out toward the sea. And he caught me staring. "This is unreal," he said.

I looked quickly away, ducking my head to hide my smile. It was hardly something to be proud of, this strange rundown castle we called home. But I was proud anyway.

"It feels … good, up here," he said. "But I always feel things more at Lúnasa, I think. Do you know much about it?"

I shook my head.

"It's pretty incredible," he said, turning to face me. "It's halfway between the summer solstice and the autumn equinox. It was this festival full of feasting and competitions, music and storytelling, sacrifices and rituals. Everything. Nothing like today's festivals."

Smoothing the paper on the thick stone parapet, I wrote,

I wish we could go. To the original one.

He laughed. "You would have liked it." He watched me as his mirth naturally abated. I liked that. His taking the time to share that with me. After a few moments, he went on. "But it wasn't all fun and merriment. It was originally started by the god Lugh as a funeral feast in honor of his stepmother, who'd died of exhaustion after clearing the plains of Ireland to grow and feed the people."

You know a lot about Celtic myth, I wrote.

He shrugged. "It's my heritage." He looked steadily at me, and his eyes felt like a kaleidoscope I couldn't climb out of. As much as I tried to regain my senses, I was lost. And I didn't want to be found. "Yours, too."

Taking one step closer, Louis reached out and tucked a loose coil of hair behind my ear.

"Why don't you ever talk, golden girl by the sea?"

I shrugged, nervously popping the cap off and back on the pen. Louis's hand moved to my chin, tipping it upward. I closed my eyes, not willing to let him determine where I looked. I would open them when I was ready. His hand moved to my neck and lay there, waiting, patient, warmly covering the place where my heartbeat pulsated. I opened my eyes.

But nothing could have prepared me for being so close to a boy with such beautiful depths to his eyes, his soul, his person.

"Can I kiss you?" he whispered.

For once it didn't matter that I had no voice. The pen still clenched in my hand like a lifeline, I nodded.

His lips were burning hot against mine, and I almost pulled away in surprise. But there was a delicious sensation pounding through me, and his other hand had curled around my back, holding me closer to him than I'd ever been to another person. All of a sudden, it didn't matter that I couldn't see his emotions like other people's. Because now I tasted him and felt him and knew him.

Everything was Louis.

That's probably why I didn't feel her approaching.

"OH MY GOD!"

I jumped away from Louis, the cold air rushing between us. Bríd stood on the threshold as the door to the roof knocked against the wall, clearly thrown open in haste. Finbar swooped out into the night sky. "I—I—"

A bright pink glow pulsated around her, slowly leaking away into a heavy black fog the longer she stared at me and Louis. Her eyes were going glassy. "I—I thought—" My gaze flew to her hand. Clasped there was a familiar sheet of creased blue paper.

She thought it was for her.

"Is this ... " Bríd looked back and forth between us, and Finbar whirled around to retreat to his girl. "Is this for her?" Bríd's gaze settled on Louis, and I looked at him for the first time since being interrupted. He looked incredibly uncomfortable, scratching his eyebrow and biting his lip. Squeezing the pen in my hand so hard it dug into my skin, I waited for him to answer.

Finally, he scratched the back of his head and stared at Bríd's feet as he nodded.

"Oh my god. Feck." Bríd breathed heavily, her cheeks aflame. On her shoulder, Finbar stepped uncomfortably from foot to foot. "I thought ... yesterday ... and then you left so abruptly. And then I found this and thought that's why ... just shy ... and ... Feck!" Dropping the poem, she turned and sprinted down the stairs, Finbar squawking after her.

Brí! I went after her, not even stopping to pick up the first love letter I'd ever gotten, nearly tripping down the stairs in my haste. I didn't know what had happened between my sister and Louis yesterday, but none of it was worth the anguish and embarrassment I felt emanating from my wild, confident sister now.

She wasn't in her room, and I found her in the kitchen, bustling around making tea. Because that's what the Irish did in times like these.

I felt so embarrassed, so naked and stripped open for all to see as I stepped into the kitchen and approached her. Faolan jumped up and ran to me, rubbing against my legs looking for a pet, but I didn't have time for him.

"I'm sorry," I signed to Bríd around the pen still clutched in my hand.

"Rí, stop." She sighed, setting down the kettle. "It's not your fault." The dark energy around her swirled up into a storm. "It's his."

Louis stood behind me, awkwardly lingering in the doorway. He had the intelligence not to respond to such an accusation from Bríd.

"How is it his fault?" I signed.

"Fault, fault," Finbar crooned.

"He played us, like. Can't you see that, Rí?"

"What?" Louis stammered. "I—"

"What was last night about?" Bríd shouted, turning on him. Clouds swirled around her, anger personified, enclosing poor Finbar as he shuffled nervously back and forth on her shoulder. But beneath the bluster, that familiar murky shadow hung from her shoulders, manifest loneliness, while a dull pulse beat under it all like a broken heart. "And then moving in on her? You've been flirting with the both of us since the day we met you!"

I felt something in me shifting. A little piece of Bríd's anger that I'd taken for my own.

"Bríd," Louis said calmly, "I'm sorry—"

"No!" she interrupted.

"No! No!" Finbar screeched.

"You do not get to woo me like some knight in shining armor and then move in on my sister!"

I held that piece of anger and worked it like clay, flattening it, then building it up, bigger and bigger.

"Why did you do it?" Bríd barreled on. "Did you want something from us? Or was it just the typical feckin' lad reasons?"

I let out a strangled scream.

Bríd, Finbar, and Louis all turned to me in surprise. Faolan nudged my palm with his wet nose.

"You only think he played us because you can't imagine someone liking me," I signed, glaring at Bríd. *"Really liking me. At least not when you're around."*

Bríd's mouth fell open, and the clouds around her stilled. "That is not … How could you say that?"

Louis looked on, helpless.

"Easy. Because it's true," I signed. *"You think any boy who likes me must be pretending. Admit it."*

The clouds whipped into a frenzy. "That's not true, and I cannot believe you're taking his side!" Tears were pooling in her eyes, and Finbar let out a plaintive coo. "He played us, Rí! You don't know the things I told him last night! Because he was being so feckin' nice! Such a feckin' flirt! And now I know it was all some ploy."

"It wasn't—"

"Shut it, you eejit!" Bríd roared at Louis.

He sighed and dropped his face in his hands. I only stared at my sister. Faolan whined.

"I told him everything, Rí!" she yelled. "Everything! I showed him the feckin' pen, like! I told him things I've never even told you! That's right." She shook her head and went quiet. "I told him things I wouldn't even tell you."

Tears stung my eyes. How had my first kiss gone so very wrong?

"Why?" I signed.

"Because he was being such a feckin' gentleman!" Bríd yelled. "Because … Because I was lonely!"

sabaitéireacht
SABOTAGE

a i d a n

"That sounds like a fight," I said.

Moira sighed. "If Bríd's even picking fights with Ríona now, she must be in a real mood."

"We should go down there."

She groaned and threw her head against the back of the couch. "Do we have to? Could we not let them battle it out, like the olden days? It'd be like a real castle again, two brave maidens coming to blows."

I laughed. "You don't mean that, and you know it." She was already standing.

"Of course I don't. Because I *care* about them, or something. It gets old, you know, being the mother." And the way she said it, that last sentence, told me she wasn't joking.

Bríd, Ríona, and that bastard Louis were in a tense standoff in the

kitchen. Finbar was nervously moving around his girl's shoulders while Faolan sat at Ríona's feet, nudging her hand with his wet nose.

Moira marched straight across the room to the stove and whirled around, folding her arms across her chest. "What's going on here?" She anxiously looked around the room.

Finbar squawked and took flight — right at Louis's face.

The guy threw his arms up in protection, but Ríona got there first, grabbing Finbar out of the air.

"Don't touch him!" Bríd snapped, darting forward and grabbing her bird from her sister's hands.

I joined Moira at the stove, watching Louis carefully. Moira was right in deducing that I had no good reason not to like the guy. But it didn't change the fact that I didn't. And neither, apparently, did Finbar. Yet Faolan still stood placidly at Ríona's side. That was unusual. From what I'd seen in the castle, Faolan was the most protective, the leeriest of outsiders, while Finbar was an easy enough one to win over. So how had Louis convinced the wolf he was no danger to these girls but not the bird?

"Somebody better tell me what is going on," Moira demanded.

"Nothing!" Bríd snapped, setting her bird back on her shoulder. "Jaysus, Moira, do you have to be at the center of everything?" Finbar, clearly angry with her, swooped away and settled on the stone hearth just beside me.

"Only when you all are acting like children!" Moira yelled back.

"Oh, do children go shifting all over the place?" Bríd asked.

"What?" Moira looked from Bríd to Ríona and back. "Who's shifting who?"

"Jaysus, when did we become a feckin' soap opera?" Bríd groaned.

It took me a moment to realize the itch I'd felt on my hand wasn't an itch at all. When Finbar painfully dug his beak into my hand, I gathered he wanted my attention. He had a piece of blue paper clasped in his beak.

I took it and unfolded it, scanning it quickly. Some bad poetry was scrawled on it in messy handwriting. Sighing, I rolled my eyes. Poetry? Really? This was one serious Romeo we had here. Was this the source of the current fight unfolding here between sisters? Which one of them was the "golden girl by the sea"?

I turned to show the poem to Moira, but something made me pause. Something, a truth, a realization, was niggling at my brain. But I couldn't make it take clear shape.

"Is this a fight about him?" Moira asked, pointing at Louis. "Because that would be such a waste of your time."

"Oh, you're one to talk, Moira!" Bríd yelled.

It was the As. I stared at the poem. I'd seen that old-fashioned style of lowercase *a* before. Recently.

In their father's letter.

This handwriting looked exactly like the handwriting in the letter from the girls' father. And only one person had been here the day it appeared. Well, not a person.

Finbar squawked.

I looked up. Louis stood near the door with a careful look of appropriate shame on his face. I had no time to waste.

"You wrote the letter!" I yelled at him.

Everyone went silent. They stared at me. I glared at Louis.

"Me?" Louis said, his eyes darting around. "What are you talking about?" His eyes flew to the paper in my hand. "Oh, that? Yes, I wrote that."

"No." I shook my head. "That letter from their father. It was a forgery. I knew it. And I didn't like you. Not one bit. But I didn't know why."

"What are you talking about?" Louis said, his face scrunched up in a pretty good imitation of confusion.

Bríd was looking back and forth between Moira and me. "Yeah, what is he talking about, like?"

I held up the paper. "This stupid poem he wrote, to one of them"—I nodded at Bríd and Ríona—"the handwriting looks exactly like the handwriting in your dad's letter."

Louis scoffed. "It's all the same alphabet, you know. Plenty of people write it alike."

I shoved the poem at Moira. Her eyes flew over the words, and she blanched. Bríd ran to a drawer in the kitchen counter, pulled a piece of paper out of it, and dashed to Moira. They looked between the two, their faces full of confusion.

Bríd rubbed her eyes. "I … I thought this was Dad's handwriting," Moira murmured, squinting at the letter. "But it's the same as the poem …" Finally, they looked up, horror apparent on each girl's face.

"Why did you feckin' forge a letter from our dad?" Bríd yelled at Louis, as Moira shouted, "*How?*"

"Dad! Dad!" Finbar screeched.

Ríona looked positively terrified. She took a step back, and I thought she was going to run for it, but she didn't. She just stood there, staring at Louis, twisting her fingers around a pen in her hands.

"I have no idea what you're talking about!" Louis yelled.

"Yes, you do!" Bríd shook her head, brandishing their father's letter in her hand. "This showed up after you left us at Sheehan's farm. I-I don't know how you know what our dad's handwriting looks like, but-but you clearly know how to forge it! This poem is written in exactly the same way! Why did you run back here with a forged letter while we were distracted with Sheehan? Why did you want us to stay here?"

"I-I don't know what you're talking about," Louis said. "I didn't do it."

Ríona stepped forward, shaking like a leaf, and we all looked at her. She held the pen out to Louis.

He stared at it.

"What … What do you want me to do with that?" he asked.

"Write it down," Bríd said, stepping forward. "You know what the pen does. So write down that you didn't forge that letter."

Louis's face dropped. "No," he said firmly.

"Why? Because you're lying?"

"No!" Louis yelled. "Because this is ridiculous, and I don't deserve—"

"*You* don't deserve?" I shouted, surprised by my own outburst. "They don't deserve whatever you're doing to them!"

"I … I didn't do this, and I don't know why you think someone would forge a letter from your dad—"

"Write it down, Louis," Bríd said. "Or leave."

"Leave!" Finbar repeated.

Louis swallowed and looked at the floor.

After nearly half a minute of full silence, it was Ríona who walked to the kitchen door, unlocked it for the first time in days, and opened it wide.

"Leave! Leave!" Finbar squawked.

Louis shook his head and walked out.

deireadh leis

AN END TO IT

louis

Damnit. Damnit. Damnit. They'd backed me into a corner. I'd seen what that pen could do. It would have revealed my lies in a moment. What was I supposed to do?

And why did I feel so irrevocably *sad*? Not mad, frustrated, angry that I'd failed in this mission I'd been training for for so long. No, I felt …

Stop it. I shook my head. *Stop it.*

Taking a deep breath, I opened the front door to the Sheehans' and headed for the stairs. Hoping to keep Conry occupied while I finished my mission here — and to keep him safe from the henchman who now knew where to find him — I'd sent him off into the fields with Sheehan for the day. It was still early, and neither Sheehan and Conry nor Mrs. Sheehan would be home for hours yet. That would give me plenty of time to regroup. To plan.

To figure out why I felt so awful.

I sighed. I could not be falling for the Morrigu. That wasn't an option. And besides, it probably had something to do with who she was. That was it. And the emotion of sharing my words with her … It had been years — no, centuries, since I'd shared my poetry with anyone. But Medb's stupid henchman had made me panic. He'd made me think I needed an elaborate plan. Something good. Emotional. So I'd done it.

I wished I hadn't. As I opened the door to my room, sunlight streamed in through the window.

This time, I saw the henchman immediately.

I closed the door behind me. "Why are you here? I need to be alone. I need to come up with another plan—"

"You're done," the henchman said, standing. "You've been unassigned this mission." He pulled a shiny blade out of his long leather coat.

"What?" I breathed, backing against the closed door.

"I'm sorry, laddie, but I have to kill ya now." He advanced at a leisurely pace, like he was just going for a stroll.

"B-But I'm sworn to secrecy!" I shouted, shoving up the sleeve of my hoodie. "You know I can't say a word while the mark lasts! Why would she need me gone?"

"It's never a good idea to expect a queen to act within reason."

"Please!" I shouted. "I'm not a threat! I couldn't say anything about this entire endeavor, even if I wanted to!"

The henchman didn't even glance at my triskele mark. "I have orders," he said simply.

I ducked, but his giant hand clamped around my neck and pulled me upright.

"Why?" I shouted. "Why would she do this?"

"A boyo like yourself should never have gotten involved with a bird like her." His fist squeezed and he brought the blade to my throat. My eyes darted desperately around the room, searching for something, anything, to wield as a sword. It had been many decades since I'd been in top form, and the spear had always been my strong suit, but finding a makeshift weapon was my only hope. I'd never be able to fight him off with strength alone.

I clawed and scraped at his arm around my neck. But it was no use. He was three times the size of me, and my throat was beginning to constrict.

And then I felt it. The stirring of warmth in my veins.

It was Lúnasa.

Gripping his arm with all my strength, I took a deep breath as best I could and let out a primal scream.

Nothing happened at first. And then, I felt it, cold and sharp and solid in my hand. *Fragarach*. The Answerer. I hadn't called him forth in decades.

The henchman was too close for me to get a stab in, so I swung the sword up and brought it down on his temple. The man roared and let go of me. Taking a deep breath, I stepped forward and brought the broadside down on his head once again. I was steeling myself for the killing blow when the man bent forward and toppled to the ground, unconscious.

The hilt was ice-cold in my hand. I shook my head.

It had been nearly a century since I'd killed. And what did it matter if this man lived? There would be a hundred more where he'd come from. Besides, I'd be gone before he woke.

Shoving the sword inside my hoodie as best I could, I dashed for the door.

I flew down the stairs, bolted out the front door, and shouted for Conry. He had to hear me. He was somewhere out in the fields. Running madly, I called him in every manner I'd ever known, in tongues I hadn't used in epochs, and with the deepest reaches of my being. But the ways were old and I was tired.

"CONRY!" I screamed at the top of my lungs. Finally, he came bounding out from behind the farmhouse, and I ran, not caring what Sheehan would think when he found us both gone. I ran and ran, Conry at my heels. We ran all the way back to the castle, my breaths ripping through me, my throat on fire. I wasn't ready to die.

But I couldn't run from Medb. Not now. Not ever. She would find me. And she would make me pay for failing her. Before then, I would have to reckon myself with the end. No, I couldn't run from Medb. But I could deprive her of her most precious quarry.

na ḣaos sí

THE AOS SÍ

b r í d

The kitchen window rattled open and a sword flew into the kitchen, skidding across the flagstone floor.

"What the—?"

Louis was right behind it, panting heavily.

"What are you doing here?" Moira thundered, advancing on him at once as Finbar took flight. I grabbed him out of the air before he could make matters worse.

Louis put both hands up where he crouched on the kitchen counter. "You all are in danger," Louis said, "and I'm here to tell you why."

We stared at him. Did he truly know? Or was this another ploy of some kind?

His hound clamored awkwardly through the window frame after him, and across the room, Faolan jumped to his feet, a growl low in his

throat. He didn't advance, but Ríona put a hand on his neck just in case. She still clutched the oil lamp to her chest. She'd been sitting with it while we all paced around the kitchen, fighting. But now the lamp flashed so quickly, it was nearly a constant light. Aidan stood near the stove, his critical eyes on Louis. We'd been here in the kitchen since he'd left, yelling at each other and generally getting nowhere, so if he truly had some glimmer of truth to reveal, we needed it. Badly. But how could we trust him?

"Okay, go on then," Moira said, turning to Louis.

"Wait, wait," I said, my hands up.

"Wait!" Finbar squawked. Stroking his head, I carefully placed him back on my shoulder.

"I don't believe him," I said, marching angrily to the middle of the room. "What I want to know is how he managed to forge a letter in Dad's handwriting!" I glared at Louis. "Have you seen him? Do you know where he is? Are you involved in the reason he hasn't come home?"

Louis slid off the counter and grabbed the sword. "Did you miss the part where I said you are in *danger*?" he repeated, brandishing the sword across the kitchen. His dog, Conry, slipped and slid to the floor in an ungraceful dance of paws on stone.

"Do you or do you not know where our father is?" I repeated.

"Of course I don't!" Louis snapped. Every so often, he rubbed a hand over his tattooed forearm as if it hurt. "I forged the letter with a simple confoundment spell, to make you three fail to see what I didn't want you to. But I bloody forgot about *him*." He glared at Aidan. "And I certainly didn't expect things to take so long it would wear off."

"A *what?*" Moira breathed.

"Did you say *spell?*" I whispered.

"I can't believe you don't know what you are!" Louis cried. "Don't you feel it? Know it in your soul? I always have."

"What are you talking about?" Moira demanded.

"Gah!" Louis let out a primal scream. Finbar flapped his wings, matching Louis's noise with an earsplitting caw. It was the first time I'd seen Louis lose even the tiniest bit of control. I glanced at Moira, who was looking at Aidan. Ríona stared at Louis, her eyes narrowed. "I can't tell you!" Louis shrieked. "I swear, I can't tell you!" He pushed up the sleeve on the arm gripping the sword and held his forearm out to us.

A gray symbol was tattooed there, but it meant nothing to me.

"You have a tattoo?" Moira said lamely.

"It's not a tattoo! It's the mark of a triskele oath. It prevents me from revealing the secret I've been sworn to protect. I swear it."

We all stared at him. I was the first to regain my senses — and let out a disbelieving laugh. "What are you on about?" I demanded. But nobody answered me as they all turned to watch Ríona dash across the room.

"What are you doing, Rí?" Moira asked.

Ríona walked right up to Louis and held out a pen. No, not just any pen. The truth pen.

"Yes!" Moira cried. "Write down a lie about who we are." She crossed her arms over her chest, a challenge. "The pen will change it to the truth."

Louis looked at the pen in Ríona's proffered hand for a long moment. Then he looked at her face. She watched him intently.

I don't know what her eyes told him, but he finally put his sword down and reached out to take the pen from Ríona. Moira grabbed Dad's letter, which still sat on the table, and flipped it over. Louis hesitated only a moment, then stepped forward and pressed the nib to the paper. We all gathered around him, our eyes glued to the paper.

You, Louis wrote quickly, *are—*

As the letters began to rearrange themselves to form some truth we couldn't fathom, a strangled scream pierced my ears. The pen dropped from Louis's hand as he bent forward, his left hand grasping his tattooed forearm. Ríona reached out to him, but he let out such a terrible screech we all recoiled.

"What's the matter?" Moira cried, wringing her hands. "Are you okay?

Teeth clenched, Louis finally moved his hand, and we could see the triskele glowing a bright, flickering red. As if it were on fire.

"Feck!" I yelped as Ríona whimpered and Moira gasped. Aidan had his hand over his mouth. Louis only panted through the pain.

"Louis," Moira breathed. "Who did this to you?"

"I did it to myself," he said simply.

Ríona stepped forward again, and this time, she put a hand on his. As she rubbed the back of his hand with her thumb, he relaxed, and his breathing slowed. The mark appeared to be dulling, the angry red fading.

"You called it a triskele," I said quietly. "What is that?"

"It's the mark of the triskele oath," he corrected me quietly. "It protects the secret I've been sworn to keep. I should've known better." He nodded at the pen. "That won't work. Ancient magic isn't so uncomplicated. Why would it be? The *aos sí* are the ancestors of Ireland, the spirits of nature, the gods and goddesses of old."

Ríona signed something. "She's read about them," Moira said, for Aidan's sake.

"But what does all that mean to us?" I asked.

"I can't tell you," Louis said steadily. He took a deep breath and stood tall once again, picking up his sword and holding it at his side. "But I know someone who can. You have to come with me."

"What? No," Moira said firmly. "We're not trusting you that easily."

My eyes darted to his forearm. The edges of the mark were still red. It's not like he could have forged *that*.

"Are you saying the *aos sí* are related to the reason the girls are in trouble?" Aidan asked Louis. Moira's head snapped in Aidan's direction. I could hardly believe the boy who'd been so against letting Louis into the castle at all could be entertaining the idea that he was being truthful now.

Louis pressed his lips firmly together and stared at Aidan, annoyed. "I. Can't. Say."

Aidan stared back. At long last, he said, "I believe him."

"What?" Moira gasped. My heart began to beat painfully fast. What was going on? Were these boys in league with each other? I'd seen what Aidan would bring upon my sister; was his disapproval of Louis all an act? Had they planned all this?

I looked at Louis. At the boy I'd almost kissed last night. There was a reason I'd felt safe enough to tell him all my secrets. But then he'd gone off with my sister. Neither of these boys were to be trusted.

"I know there's someone nearby who can answer your questions," Louis said, looking at Moira now. "Just come with me—"

"No," Moira said. "We're not leaving the castle."

"Please," Louis said. "A *bean nighe* can answer any question you pose her, and I know there's one nearby. She—"

The oil lamp crashed to the floor.

We all turned to Ríona. She stood, her hands frozen in midair. Whining, Faolan licked her palm, trying to bring her back to reality.

"What is it, Ríona?" Moira asked, hurrying to her side.

Ríona swallowed. She stared at Louis. Shook her head. Bent to pick up the oil lamp.

"No, Moira is right," Aidan said, stepping forward. "They're not going anywhere with you."

"What?" I breathed, looking around at the madness unfolding before me. "You just said you feckin' trusted him!"

"What? What?" Finbar shrieked.

"I … I just don't think it's a good idea," Aidan stammered.

Moira's eyes were glued to Ríona, full of worry. "What is a *bean nighe*?" she demanded of Louis.

Did Ríona know? Is that what had scared her? She certainly read more storybooks and legends than either Moira or myself.

"She's a spirit, one of the washerwomen, a shade who can answer any three questions you pose her," Louis babbled. "You can ask her anything. They know all that happens or will happen on this land."

I expected some reaction from Moira — a scoff, an admonition. Instead, she said, "Ríona? Bríd?"

My heart pounded. What if Louis was telling the truth? What if this was his gesture of reconciliation?

"Ríona? Bríd?" Finbar cawed.

And what if there really was a creature that could answer our questions? Our three most burning, desperate questions?

"Why should we believe you now?" I asked. "After you forged a letter from our father to keep us here like sitting ducks?"

Louis swallowed and glanced down. He placed his sword on the table and stepped forward, unzipping his hoodie halfway. Then he pulled his shirt collar away from his neck and met my eyes.

There were dark purple marks ringing his neck. Moira gasped, and Ríona smacked a hand over her mouth. There was a thin line of red just above Louis's Adam's apple. It looked like a fresh cut.

"Somebody tried to kill me tonight," he said.

"Why?" I breathed.

Louis shook his head. "I can't tell you."

"Feck," I muttered, my thoughts racing. "Are they coming for us?"

Louis zipped up his hoodie. "I can't tell you," he said so softly, it was almost a whisper.

But that was answer enough. We needed to know who was coming for us and why. We needed answers, and whether it was really some binding spell or just his own will, we weren't going to get them from Louis.

"This … This spirit … " I said. "We can ask her anything?"

"Anything," Louis promised. "But … there is a catch," he added quietly. We waited. "After she answers your questions, you must answer a single one of hers. And should you lie … should you respond with the smallest shred of untruth … terrible things will happen. Fate will come for you, but you won't know where or when. Such is the promise of the *bean nighe*."

"No," Aidan said. "No way."

Silence fell on the room.

"She'll answer anything we ask?" Moira repeated.

Louis took a deep breath and nodded.

"Anything!" Finbar crowed.

Moira turned to us. "*Oya.* Let's go."

an bean nighe
THE BEAN NIGHE

m o i r a

Louis led us down the Killeen. Downstream, it twisted across the rustyback and disappeared into the woods. That was precisely where Louis was leading us now, his sword held aloft in front of him. The last of the sun glinted off it, turning it golden.

"We shouldn't be doing this," Aidan murmured. "What if this is exactly what your attackers are waiting for?"

"How else are we going to get all our questions answered?" I whispered. "We can't stay cooped up there waiting for Dad when he's clearly not coming. He never was."

The sun was just beginning to set in earnest, leaving behind a wispy fog that was just settling in for the night. Louis was positively on edge. Every few steps he'd stop and turn in a circle, looking, listening, waiting, before leading us on again. Conry walked behind us, his big hound head constantly sweeping this way and that. Louis had made us

leave Finbar and Faolan at home so we could move as soundlessly as possible. To my surprise, Bríd and Ríona both agreed.

It was just after we'd entered the forest that I spotted her up ahead. A woman in rags, moving about near the stream. Her black hair fell down her back in tight corkscrew curls. Through the fog, she turned, and the last rays of the dying sun lit her face, her dark skin glowing in earnest.

My heart stopped.

Ríona cried out.

Bríd screamed.

Our mother stood before us.

"Shhh!" Louis hissed, dancing around us, his sword drawn as he tried to cover every direction. But we wouldn't have noticed if a horde of attackers descended upon us then.

"Mam!" Bríd cried and ran for her.

I beat her there. Our mother stood, her face a mask of placid calm, but her arms held wide. I hurtled into them. And passed through her like she was made of smoke.

"Moira," Aidan said, a gentle hand on my shoulder. "It's just a spirit." Behind him, Louis stood staring, alarm apparent on his face. He didn't know. He didn't know our connection to her.

Tears rushed silently down Ríona's face, but Bríd sobbed outright as they stood in front of this ghost, this spirit of the woman who had loved us and raised us and made us who we were. The woman we'd missed every day since her parting.

And she stood there, looking as solid as the trees around us, emotionless and tranquil. Almost as if we were strangers.

"Ríona," I whispered, remembering her reaction in the kitchen. "Did you know?"

I had to tear my eyes from the vision in front of me to get Ríona's answer. She shook her head violently. *"I've read about the bean nighe,"* she signed, her fingers flying. *"But I never dreamed ..."* She wiped her eyes. *"It used to be said they were the spirits of women who'd died in childbirth. They were seen near streams, washing bloody clothing. But that was back when people didn't understand death and ... and I never dreamed ... I never dreamed—"*

"I know, I know." I took her into my arms. Tears were streaming down her face so hard I was sure she couldn't see any longer. Aidan stood behind us, his face in his hands. He'd tried to prevent us from coming here. Was that because he'd known what we'd find?

"You must do this quickly," Louis hissed, clutching his sword. Conry circled us obediently, his great paws crunching leaves and twigs as he moved steadily around and around.

"Moira," Bríd moaned between sobs, a pathetic plea.

"Okay," I said, releasing Ríona and stepping forward. "First question. Is ... Is Dad alive?"

The spirit of our mother smiled, and it felt so familiar, so real, I almost ran into her arms again. "Yes, *Kehinde.*"

Bríd let out a strangled howl of relief, but I struggled to breathe for the pain lancing through my chest. *Kehinde.* The name given to the second of twins. I'd forgotten she'd called me that. She'd had a special name for each of us. And her voice — that soothing pitch that I heard in my heart every day, the smooth blend of Irish accented with the special cadence of her own parents' Yoruba language. I breathed in deeply, half-expecting to smell coconut oil, but it was only dirt and moss and rotting wood that reached my nostrils.

"What are we?" Bríd piped up, wiping her eyes.

Our mother turned to her with a fond look. "The Morrigan runs through your veins, *Taiwo*."

"The wha—"

"Stop!" I shouted, lest that be our third question. Bríd snapped her mouth shut. Beside me, Ríona began to shake anew. Did she know what in the world that was? The Morrigan? I didn't have time to ask her. We had one question left, and we needed to know who was after us. But we also needed to know why. How could I ask both—

"When are we going to be attacked again?" Bríd blurted out.

"Bríd!"

"Tomorrow night," Mam replied.

"No," I breathed. I spun toward Bríd. "Why did you do that? We need to know who is after us. And *why*!"

"We also need to know when we'll be feckin' fighting for our lives again!" Bríd snapped.

"Remember," Louis said sharply, "she's not done!"

Sure enough, our mother was gliding forward. "A question I must now ask each of you, the sisters three."

an chead ceist
THE FIRST QUESTION

a i d a n

The *bean nighe* turned to Ríona and looked at her for several long moments as the girl shook. We never should have come. I should have tried harder to keep them away. This wasn't right.

"Ríona," the shade said, "*Eta Oko*. Can you speak yet?"

Sniffling, Ríona shook her head, tears glistening in her eyes. I looked away. It felt like a moment I shouldn't see. But one word kept rippling over me: *yet*.

an dara ceist
THE SECOND QUESTION

aidan

Moira had a watery smile on her face as the *bean nighe* turned to her.

"*Kehinde*," the woman said. "Do you still have your *fíorláir*?"

The smile faded from Moira's face. She looked to Bríd and Ríona, who both shook their heads, Bríd shrugging.

"The True Mare," Louis said softly. He'd stopped circling us with the *bean nighe*'s promise that the girls were safe until tomorrow. "The seventh filly born to a mare with no colts. She's lucky. Safe from enchantment or nefarious intervention. Blessed, as it were. And that protection is bestowed on any who ride her."

"What?" Moira murmured.

"Your pony," Louis said softly.

"Bó," Moira breathed. She turned back to the shade in a daze and nodded. "Yes."

an triú ceist
THE THIRD QUESTION

a i d a n

The *bean nighe* turned once more, this time to the third sister. Bríd smiled at her through her tears.

"*Taiwo*," the *bean nighe* said. "Have you told your sisters what you see in your sleep?"

Tears leaked from the corners of Bríd's wide eyes. She stared, unblinking, at the shade for a moment, and when her glance shot to Moira, neither of her sisters were looking. They couldn't tear their eyes from the likeness of their mother.

At long last, Bríd murmured, "Yes."

And neither sister questioned her. Why would they? Even I could see — they trusted each other implicitly. As absolutely as the mind trusts the eye. Only I saw fresh sobs wrack Bríd's body anew.

ag coinneáil bigil
KEEPING VIGIL

ríona

The cold seeped into me through the ground, but I didn't mind. It felt good to be cooled as everything in me burned. She looked so real. So solid. So like her as she moved about the bank of the Killeen, washing rags in the freezing water. I yearned to reach out and touch her, but I knew if I felt what Moira had, it would ruin the illusion. From three feet away, I could pretend she was really there.

"We just want to watch her," Moira explained gently to Aidan. She spoke calmly, but a deep red cloud enveloped her, swirling softly, obscuring her features every now and again. And I understood her melancholic confusion. Having glimpsed our mother, even if it was just a spirit, we couldn't let her out of our sight. Not yet. I wasn't sure I ever could.

"No," Aidan said. "No! You can't just sit out here, with no defenses. You're safer in the castle." His split aura was as separate as

ever, two living, moving energies swirling around him. But tonight, both were terrified.

Bríd was being surprisingly calm, sitting a few feet away from me on the bank of the river. Her energy was nearly nonexistent, just a thick black fog sitting, unmoving, around her, nearly making her blend in with the gray mist. I wondered if she was lost in her dreams. Maybe they troubled her more than we knew. Maybe that's why Mam had asked. Bríd had never shied away from telling us about the things that woke her, screaming, in the middle of the night. She'd seen Dad in trouble, more than once. Was Mam trying to convince us to go after him?

"It's too dangerous!" Aidan insisted.

"You heard her," Moira said, turning away from him. "Nobody's coming for us until tomorrow."

Aidan scoffed and turned to Louis. "Would you help me out here?"

"It is safer in the castle," Louis admitted. He still gripped his sword like it was another limb, but he didn't hold it at the ready. I might not have been able to see his emotions, but it was clear enough. For his part, he believed the *bean nighe*'s prediction that we were safe until tomorrow. Even Conry sat placidly at his feet.

Moira walked to the other side of the *bean nighe* and sat on the cold ground, drawing her knees to her chest. "You all have been calling the shots long enough," she said quietly. "This isn't up to you."

Aidan heaved an angry sigh but said nothing else. The boys faded away completely the longer I watched her — our mother — move with the same easy grace she'd had in life. But there was something else that cracked the illusion that my mother stood before me once again. Hers were the first thoughts and emotions I'd ever felt outside myself. And they'd always come to me, stronger and sharper and more vivid than others'. I'd felt her more keenly, all the time our lives had overlapped. But now?

Now I felt nothing.

"Rí," Moira said, not taking her eyes from our mother. "What's the Morrigan?"

I had no idea. None of the books I'd read had taught me that. I shrugged.

"Louis?" Moira asked hopefully.

He held up his forearm emblazoned with the triskele and shook his head. "You know I can't tell you that."

scail

A SHADOW

moira

Aidan forced us back to the castle as soon as the light poked through the trees of the forest. Ríona had fallen asleep on the cold bank of the river, but Bríd and I had sat, staring, for all the long hours that the *bean nighe* moved, silently, continuously, in her morbid eternal work.

When we finally woke Ríona and began to walk away, stopping to look back every few feet, the *bean nighe* didn't even glance at us. And the moment we walked through the door at home, the boys began to prepare the castle like a proper fortification. As if we were going to battle with an army half the size of Ireland.

How had our lives come to this?

I felt drained, too tired and empty to fortify my childhood home for an attack. But there was one thing I needed to know.

"Aidan," I said, stopping him as he hurried past me with a broken wooden chair from the storage room.

"Hmm?" He tried to keep walking, but I pulled him back.

"I need to ask you something," I said.

"What is it?" he asked, putting a hand on my arm, concern etched on his face. He cared about me. He truly did. But that didn't change what I had to ask.

"Did you know she was there? The *bean nighe*? *Abeg*, don't lie to me. Is that why you didn't want us to go down there?"

The words hung between us, unanswered, as Aidan looked at the dusty flagstone.

Finally, he nodded. "Yeah."

"Did you know … she was our mother?" I asked breathlessly.

Sighing, he nodded again. "When I was wandering that first day I came back to land, I saw her down by the river, and I knew what she was. I'd heard rumors of them … out there. And then I saw the pictures upstairs, of your mom, and I put two and two together."

The world seemed to have gone silent. I could no longer hear the others pushing things around and shouting at each other. No, all I could hear and see and feel was Aidan. Aidan and the weight of his lies. Our mother had been down there, just a stone's throw from us. He knew, and he hadn't told us.

"How could you keep that from me?" I whispered.

"Moira," he said, grabbing both my arms, "that is not your mom. That is just a shadow of her. You can't—"

"I would gladly take the shadow!" I yelled. "How could you not understand that?"

"Moira—"

"No!" I ripped out of his arms, the tears welling in my eyes. "You don't get to decide whether I should see the most important person in my life who has been gone for years!" I could feel the others staring now, but I couldn't stop. "How could you think that's your decision to make? How could you possibly understand? Do you know what it's like to lose your mother?"

Aidan sighed heavily, his lips pressed firmly together. "Yes." Of course. I realized my mistake too late. Aidan had been raised by people who didn't even know what he was. He'd told me all about his birth mother and father.

He shook his head. "Without ever really knowing her, I lost my mother."

Stepping close to me, he took my hand. "And you're right. I would give anything to have just a shadow of her."

an bréag

THE LIE

ríona

The oil lamp began to flash. I was the first to notice.

"If we only had something to bar the door the way it was meant to be," Moira was saying as she paced back and forth across the sitting room.

Trembling, I ran to the window.

A full moon illuminated the rustyback, shedding light on the shadows. And that was the only reason I could see them, down by the edge of the forest.

Three dark figures atop three massive horses.

They stood in a line, watching the castle, waiting. But waiting for what?

Faolan threw back his head and let out an earsplitting howl.

"Ríona?" Moira was at my side first, then Aidan and Louis, sword in hand. But Bríd stayed seated on the arm of the couch, her foot

tapping incessantly against the floor, the black cloud around her swirling ominously. The next moment, the men began to ride, flat-out, for the castle.

"Oh my God," Moira breathed.

"Shit," Aidan muttered.

"Come on!" Louis called, dashing away from the window. "Let's take up position!" He'd already outlined that he, Conry, Aidan, and Moira would be stationed downstairs with Faolan and Bó while I manned the murder hole and Bríd and Finbar took to the roof to pelt the attackers with any burning objects we could acquire. At the top of the stairs, Louis took a deep breath, and I had a vision of a real warrior, a man who'd done this a thousand times before. "It's time!"

He'd only taken one step when Finbar came swooping through the room squawking and divebombing our heads.

"Finny!" Bríd yelled, finally jumping up from her stupor. "What are you doing? We know they're coming! We know!"

But Finbar wouldn't stop.

"Would you get control of your bird?" Moira yelled. "Whose side is he on, anyway?"

"Wait," Aidan called from near the window. "Look! They stopped!"

I ran back to the window as Bríd finally gained control of the fussy crow, who continued to screech nonstop. The riders pulled sharply on the horses' reins, turning them back, retreating a good distance.

"Why did they stop?" Moira breathed.

At first, it felt like a train was going past. The reverberation started in my shoes.

There was an earth-rending groan, a blood-curdling snap, and the heavens rained stone upon us.

"GET OUT!" Aidan shouted, grabbing me and Moira and dragging us toward the stairs as the castle shook. Everyone was running, but I couldn't see for the dust and debris —

FAOLAN!

I hooked an arm around the doorway and held on to free myself from Aidan and get back into the room, but I felt Faolan brush against my legs. I curled my hand into his fur and ran. There was nothing but dust in my eyes and broken stone pelting my head as we stumbled down the stairs.

I heard Moira scream for Bó from up ahead, but when I turned, Faolan's teeth bit down on my arm and yanked me away from the storage room, into the kitchen. The room was already covered with rubble and foggy with the dust of centuries as the ceiling shook.

We just have to make it to the garden.

My shin hit something solid and I nearly fell, but Faolan jumped up to steady me. Finbar screeched close overhead, going away from the exit, but the dust was making everything fuzzy and I knew I had to hurry. There was a crash, and the floor above us groaned. The timber was too old to hold for long.

Faolan's jaw bit down on my hand once again and pulled, and I stumbled, coughing, right through the doorway into fresh air. The moment my lungs took in a clean breath, my knees buckled, and I fell to the ground. With a mouthful of my jeans, Faolan dragged me through the kitchen garden as I looked desperately around.

Where is everyone?

"Rí! Get over here!"

"Get away from the castle!"

Aidan and Bríd stood in the bailey, shaken and gray with dust, as Finbar circled overhead.

Moira! Just before I could turn, she galloped past me atop a shivering Bó. There was a long red gash across her forehead. In the bailey, Moira slid off Bó's back and doubled back to me. "Louis! Did Louis get out?"

She was halfway back to the castle when Aidan shouted, "Moira, don't you dare!"

It was a stone castle. This imposing monument had survived centuries of warfare and neglect. Surely, it could withstand whatever this was …

A stone attached to a sharp piece of wood hurtled to the ground just feet from Moira.

"Once the beams go, the whole thing will crumble!" Bríd shouted.

A coughing, spluttering figure stepped out of the kitchen, a huge dog in his arms, along with his sword. He ran through the garden to the bailey and deposited Conry in the grass. Louis wiped the gray-white dust from his face, and Conry stood to shake himself. We all looked like ghosts.

"Are you okay?" Moira asked. I turned to look up at the crumbling castle, crowned as it was with a halo of fleeing bats.

Louis climbed to his feet and rounded on us, his face full of fury. "It feels charged!" he shouted, stabbing his sword to punctuate each word. "Like sorcery!"

"What?" Moira breathed beside me.

"Did any of you lie to the *bean nighe*?" Louis yelled, turning to each of us in turn. I jumped as stones the size of Faolan tumbled from the third story. "Did you lie to her?" Louis insisted.

"What-What happened—" Moira stammered, her eyes glued to the shaking walls of our home.

"DID ANY OF YOU LIE TO THE *BEAN NIGHE*?" Louis screamed over the crash of the falling castle.

"NO!" Moira screamed back. I shook my head, tears making everything go blurry.

Louis dropped his sword to his side as he turned, his chest heaving.

Nobody said anything.

I followed his gaze.

Bríd stood there, her arms wrapped around herself, tears streaming down her cheeks. And she nodded.

With a noise like thunder, the sixth floor of the castle crumpled into the fifth, and the fourth buckled into the third, enveloping the second in a puff of smoke that obscured our home's last breath of life.

laoch ó fadó
WARRIOR OF BEFORE

bríd

"WHAT DID YOU DO?" Louis bellowed.

"What?" Moira whispered. Ríona just stared. Covered with the dust of our disintegrating home, they looked like phantoms. Not like our mother, the *bean nighe*, but storybook ghosts, with wide, round eyes. Tears left tracks down Ríona's face.

"We don't have time for this!" Aidan shouted, pointing.

Across the rubble of our home, the riders approached at full speed. They split at the castle, two coming around each side and one going right through it.

"Let's go!" Louis shouted. "New plan!"

But the time for planning was up. The rider on the far right was upon us. He pulled a broadsword out of a scabbard with a loud hiss and swung it at Louis's head. Louis ducked it deftly and whistled for Conry. The dog, still gray from the castle's dust, ran up to his boy, and

Louis stepped onto his back like Conry was a horse and he a trick rider.

"What the—?" I breathed.

"Bríd!" Moira yelled.

The rider on the left had nearly caught up. I stumbled backward as Finbar took to the air and dove at the rider's face. Moira looked at me, nodded once, and slid onto Bó's back, coaxing her into a gallop. Aidan ran after them as they sprinted at the rider.

Ahead, the last attacker slowly approached, his horse carefully stepping through the rubble of our beloved castle, as though he relished the pain it must cause us. The man was big and hairy, his pale face covered in a shadow of stubble. He leered.

Ríona tugged on my arm, and I looked quickly to her. She kissed my cheek, patted Faolan, and nodded to the left of the rider. I understood her plan, but her hands were shaking as she darted away and I almost told her to stop. We had nothing. Not a weapon, not a curio to our name.

Fanning out to the right, I matched Ríona's position on the other side of the man. He tried to watch us both. I heard Moira yelling but could spare them only a glance. She led her attacker in circles, riding round him, while Aidan and Finbar pelted him with whatever they could find. To my right, I heard the clash of metal on metal, but Louis was the last person I was worried about.

The man between Ríona and me turned his horse to face me.

Looking desperately around, I caught sight of the gnarled remains of the whitethorn and blackthorn. Slipping and sliding on the detritus of our home, I ran for it, managing to break a branch off to wield in front of me like a sword. Lord help me if what they said was true —

bad luck would befall anyone who destroyed a fairy tree.

By the time I turned, the man was galloping at me. I slid through the rubble, climbing over a half wall that had been part of the kitchen and crouching behind it. To have a chance at this, I'd need to get the man off his horse.

Right, because then it would just be his sword against my feckin' stick.

The clash of Louis's sword either dealing a hefty blow or receiving one made tears spring to my eyes.

Would we get out of this alive?

Suddenly, a heavy stone pelted the man in the back, and he reared around to face Ríona, who crouched among the wreckage of what used to be the storage room, Faolan at her side. They darted sideways as the rider steered his horse toward them.

Jumping into action, I circled around the rider in the opposite direction, searching the ground for something, anything, that could be thrown, something with more weight than the feckin' stick. Anything that could be weaponized! Before he could get very near Ríona, I stooped and dug through some broken wood to pry free a large shard of broken mirror. Running as fast as I could at the attacker, I threw the shard. It sliced my flesh as it left my hand, leaving a river of blood across my palm. But it hit true.

The attacker roared and reared around again. I stumbled backward, my chest constricting painfully at the sight of the fury in his eyes. I ran as fast as I could toward the small mountain of stone that had built up over where the kitchen table used to be. But the horse's hooves, sliding and shifting on the ruins, were close behind me. I had to turn and fight or get trampled to death.

Taking in a deep breath, I turned.

Faolan jumped in front of me, snarling, and the giant horse spooked.

He reared up on his hind legs with a powerful whinny, tossing his rider. The man landed on the broken rubble of the kitchen with a crunch. Ríona ran forward and grabbed his horse's reins while Faolan attacked the man, starting with the ankles.

The man roared in pain, and I could only watch in morbid fascination. Until I heard Moira scream.

"Faolan! *Oya!*" I called. Ears perked, the dog released the man and dashed toward Moira. But Moira's foe wasn't moving as she scrambled from Bó's back. The man lay nearby, his chest heaving, blood seeping from his cloak, his face scratched beyond recognition. But that wasn't why Moira cried. Aidan lay on the ground, writhing.

My leg was wrenched out from under me, the world turned upside down, and I landed on my back — hard.

"We only need the one of you, lassie," the man croaked. He crawled across the ground. Something in him was clearly broken. But he needed only gravity and his forearm to strap me to the ground. He had the bloody piece of mirror in his hand, and he was reaching for my neck.

"Ríona!" I gasped, choking beneath his weight.

Above the man's head, Finbar circled, picking his moment to dive. But the man saw me watching. He looked up and struck out with the glass shard at Finbar's inky black chest. Finbar was knocked backward and hit the debris of the kitchen with a muffled thud.

"FINNY, NO!" I screamed. Slashing out with all my might, I tried to push the man off me, and out of the corner of my eye, I saw Finbar take flight on struggling wings.

And then I heard it.

It grew to thundering proportions before I realized it was there in the first place. A buzzing. A vibration within the very rubble of the castle.

The man looked up as a storm of bees erupted from the rubble of the storage room. And they didn't halt in their path. They descended upon us.

I covered my head with my arms, but not a single one touched me. My attacker's screams told me he wasn't so lucky. I opened my eyes. Wailing in pain, the man tried to drag himself out of the cloud, but the bees followed him like … like magic.

Behind them all stood Ríona, her eyes closed, her face tilted up toward the black night sky. The moon made her glow like the *bean nighe*.

"STOP!" It was Louis, running toward us. "Stop them before he's killed!"

Ríona's eyes snapped open, and the bees swooped away from the man in one giant cloud.

I stared at her. Louis ran forward and knelt on the man's chest. The man cried out, but Louis only flipped him over and held his hands together. "Tell us everything!" Louis growled.

Ríona ran to me, and gingerly touched my forehead. "I'm fine," I whispered. "But, Rí … were you … were you controlling them?"

Her eyes were huge and round, but she nodded, just barely, almost imperceptibly. Finbar swooped out of the sky and landed on my chest, gently pecking at my chin with his long beak. I lifted a finger to pet his silky head, but I left a little blood behind. He rubbed his head against my chin as if to reassure me. Thank feck, he was okay. Above us, the bees moved in an undulating mass over the rubble of the castle and then away toward the outer wall and the forest. We watched them disappear, and then Ríona helped me to my feet.

Louis's adversary was on the ground, unmoving. Moira stood supporting Aidan as they watched a figure on a horse gallop away down the rustyback. And before us lay the third of the trio. Louis stood and snarled down at him, "If you want to live, you'll tell us everything you know!"

The man snorted, and blood leaked out of his mouth. "Gladly."

"Who are you?" Aidan demanded, limping forward. There was a long gash along his shin.

"And why are you after us?" Moira cried. "Who sent you?"

The man chortled, blood gurgling, once again. He pointed at Louis. "Why don't you ask him?"

an fhírinne
THE TRUTH

l o u i s

"Louis, what is he talking about?"

Bríd's voice was hoarse, and there were dark bruises forming across her throat. Finbar kept one eye on her from her shoulder as she moved gingerly over the rubble.

Shaking my head, I touched the triskele on my arm. "You know I can't tell you." I sniffed and wiped my face with my sleeve, turning back to the last remaining horseman. "But he can."

The man's eyes flew open. He'd been losing consciousness. I needed to get it out of him before we lost his knowledge for good. "Tell them why you're here," I demanded, shoving my boot in his side.

He barely registered the pain but sneered at me. Turning his eyes on the girls, his grin grew. "Queen Medb offered the crown to any man in Connacht or beyond who could retrieve the Morrigu." Rolling over, he spit on the ground. It was nothing but blood. "And deliver her in

chains."

My heart stopped.

No.

That wasn't the plan.

Was he lying? Spitting again, he struggled to take in a breath. *No,* something in me said. She wouldn't trust him with her true plan. My heart took off at a gallop. What if … What if it was me she hadn't trusted?

I was supposed to convince the Morrigu to come back with me. To accept her place at the head of Ireland and help Medb reform the Ériu of old. *That* was the plan! Medb had said I needed to accomplish this before the hordes found out the Morrigu lived and came for her themselves.

I shook my head.

Had Medb herself been the one to set the hordes upon us? Did she intend to cage the Morrigu and usurp her power?

Oh, gods. What had I done?

"What crown?" Aidan asked, just as Moira wailed, "The Morrigu? Is that one of the curios? We don't have them! They're all gone!"

"No, Moira," Bríd said, her voice emotionless. "It's what the *bean nighe* said — about the Morrigan."

"Morrigan, Morrigan," Finbar repeated quietly.

The man laughed, and blood spurted through his missing tooth, the horrible sound echoing around the empty space now enclosed by the outer wall.

"Does this have to do with why our father was taken?" Moira asked, near hysterics. "Does she have our father — this Medb?"

"Is that how you found us?" Aidan asked.

"I don't know the answers you seek," the man grumbled, still sneering. It pleased him to see us panic. He raised one bloody brow. "You know, the woman once promised her daughter to over one hundred men." He laughed again, and a trickle of blood dripped down his chin. "But there are far more than that looking for you now."

Medb had used me. It was all clear to me now, spelled out in the ancient stone that lay broken at my feet.

Ríona turned to me, her eyes watery and round, her wolf winding protectively around her legs. I'd seen this girl harness her power just the smallest bit tonight. She'd used the bees as a weapon as deadly as Fragarach. Without any help, any instruction, she'd used her desperation, her fear for her sisters and her home, and she'd made magic.

After I'd been heartlessly wooing her, trying to subdue her for another's nefarious purposes, like the spineless coward I was.

"Louis," Bríd said desperately, turning to me. I felt like I couldn't breathe. "*Abeg*, don't lie to us. Are you part of this?"

How could I ever have been part of this?

Why had I believed a cruel woman like Medb could truly want to help the Morrigu return to power?

Because I'd wanted to. I'd wanted to return to the ways of old. Ríona's eyes shone with tears. The ways of old were long gone.

"Not anymore," I said, and I twisted the heel of my boot into the attacker's gut. "Is she coming here?" I asked. "Medb. Or will she wait for you lot to fail? Is that where your friend went running off to? To report back to her?"

The man groaned. His shirt was soaked red, and I knew we were short on time. "Why don't ye just give in?" he croaked. He looked at Ríona and winked at her. "If you let me go and submit, help me earn the crown, I will be kind to you."

"What crown?" Aidan snapped. "There is no royalty in Ireland!"

The attacker laughed, but it morphed into a cough that rattled his chest. Choking, he flipped onto his side and heaved. At last, he looked at Ríona, smiled, and stopped breathing.

"Louis," Moira said softly. "The *bean nighe* said the blood of the Morrigan runs through our veins. But the woman who came to the castle … she called Ríona 'Queen.'"

"That man," Bríd said, her voice choked, "he said they only needed one of us alive."

"They're after Ríona," Aidan said quietly.

I couldn't form the words or even nod, for the triskele prevented me. But I turned to Ríona. She stood frozen in place, her arms shaking, her eyes wide. Staring into her gentle face, I willed her to understand. What she was, what I'd done, what she would have to do …

Faolan threw his head back and released a primal, heart-wrenching howl at the moon.

na pleananna leaghta amach is fearr
THE BEST LAID PLANS

ríona

"I swear to you, I was misled," Louis said. He scratched at the triskele mark on his arm as though he could rip it off that way. "I will explain all to you someday. I swear it. But now — now you have to leave."

I looked around through the mist building in my eyes. Our castle lay in ruins, every piece of our lives smashed to smithereens. The once-great castle was a pile of dusty rubble. We didn't have a home anymore, and more than a hundred men were on their way to kidnap us and take us to this Queen Medb. And it was me she wanted.

We had to leave. The strangest part was that we'd been prepared to leave before — to find Dad. But not like this. This, I realized, was a different kind of leaving. This, I suddenly knew, was forever.

The truth burned through me like a fire I couldn't quench. We had

to leave. *Now.* And we no longer had a home to come back to.

"You need to split up," Louis said.

"Not a chance," Moira said, just as Aidan said, "It's the only way."

"What?" Moira rounded on him. Their energies blew furiously about them, all mixed up in one frenzy.

"I'll hold them off as long as I can," Louis said, "while you split up —"

I jerked around. "You have to come with us, Louis," Bríd said.

"No." He shook his head. "I'll only be a hindrance. They tailed me once, and I didn't even notice. I'll only bring more danger upon you."

"Well, we won't leave without you," Bríd said, crossing her arms. "Do you really want to be the reason the next band of marauders finds us here?"

He swallowed and looked to each of us in turn. He looked at me last. Though I couldn't see his thoughts or feelings, they were as clear as day in that moment. He had never known such kindness. "Why would you do that for me?" he asked.

"Because we believe you," Moira said.

"And they almost killed you, man," Aidan said.

"And we're prone to trusting people we shouldn't," Bríd said with a smile.

I only stared. But Louis caught my gaze and held it. "Then let's make a plan."

We gathered tightly around a large stone that used to form part of the base of the castle. It had survived fairly intact, and Aidan was able to rest there. "We can go to my father," he said, panting just from the journey of ten feet. "He'll help us."

"I think the girls should leave the country immediately," Louis said.

"Not happening," Moira interrupted. "We have to find Dad."

Louis sighed. "Then Ríona and I can go to Dublin to look for your father," he said, "while you all go to Aidan's on Inis Mór. That's closer, and Aidan won't be able to travel far yet."

"No," Moira said, slicing her hand through the air. "I'm not leaving Rí, not knowing what I do now."

Moira.

"Fine." Louis brushed a hand over his face. "Aidan and Ríona can go to his father with the true mare. As long as Ríona rides the mare, she'll be protected. The rest of us can try to track your father."

Moira looked skeptically at Bó, who was standing in the grass a few feet away, stamping her back legs. It was certainly difficult to believe the pony who'd lived in our field most of our lives carried such protective powers.

"I'll agree to that," Moira said.

Bríd stepped forward, her body wracked with silent sobs. I started, and Moira gasped.

"Bríd, what on Earth is wrong?" Moira stepped toward her, but Bríd backed away. Moira went white.

"M-Moira has to go with the true mare," Bríd said through sobs.

"Why?" Louis asked carefully.

"I-I—" Bríd's words were drowned in her sorrow or fear or whatever it was that hung about her in a thick cloud.

Louis looked from Bríd to Moira, realization dawning over his face. "The omen."

"The what?" Aidan asked, distraught.

"The Blood Omen." Louis turned to look at Bó. "The mare cried tears of blood. I thought she belonged to Bríd." He glanced from sister to sister, his eyes finally resting on me. He swallowed. "The blood tears of a mare foretell the death of her rider."

"What?" Aidan cried. Moira went paler still.

"Moira," Bríd sobbed. "I-I see things in my dreams. Horrible things!"

"What did you see?" Moira asked, her voice barely a whisper.

"I saw you … " Bríd shook her head. "I saw you *die*." Bríd fell to her knees, dislodging Finbar, who hopped to the ground and cawed pitifully. Bríd dropped her face into her hands. "And I had dreams like this before."

The air around Moira was still and gray, and I wanted to reach through it to touch her, but my brain was caught up in trying to force Bríd's words to make sense. They just wouldn't sink in far enough for me to grasp them. Was Bríd saying she had predicted Moira's death?

Moira looked at Aidan, who reached out and squeezed her hand. "We don't know that it's something that's going to come true," he said softly.

"It's … It's happened before!" Bríd cried.

"When?" Moira whispered. But we all knew the answer.

"I saw Mam die in childbirth," she wailed, "before it ever happened." Bríd shook her head, her black hair whipping around her head. "It was just a dream, and I was just a feckin' child! I didn't know what I was seeing!"

My hands were shaking again, and I wasn't sure they'd ever stop.

"I couldn't tell you," Bríd moaned. "I-I couldn't tell any of you!"

Finbar gave a piteous coo, and we stood there, a pathetic tableau that seemed destined to stand here in our own sorrow, amid the wreckage of centuries, until the very end of time itself.

Eventually, Bríd's sobs died into great, heaving breaths.

At long last, Louis cleared his throat. "We need to leave here," he said gently.

Moira nodded. She sniffed and stepped forward. "We're not splitting up," she said with finality. "We'll go to Aidan's father to see if he can help us. Then we'll look for Dad. After that … Well, we'll have to see."

We'd have to see who was still alive.

Aidan and Louis both nodded. A battle with Moira wouldn't be won. Not now.

"Do ye hate me?" Bríd asked, her shoulders shaking with repressed sobs as she looked up from the rubble of the place where we'd spent our entire lives.

Moira took Bríd by the elbows and helped her stand. Then she embraced her, and I stepped forward to take them both into my arms.

"We could never hate you, Bríd," Moira whispered within our tight circle, our tiny world that was about to crack open and never be ours again. "We're your sisters."

With an arm around each of us, Moira steered us over the broken debris of our castle. Faolan pressed close to my legs, Finbar resettled on Bríd's shoulder, and Bó circled ahead of us. Moira guided us through the bailey, over the outer wall, and down the rustyback hill for good.

imeacht an dia atá ar lár
FLIGHT OF THE FALLEN GOD

m e d b

The man looked at his feet, and I fought the distinct urge to have him decapitated.

"What do you mean he failed?" I shouted. My voice reverberated around the cold chamber.

"When Walsh didn't return in a timely manner, Your Majesty, I went after him." The man was speaking to the floor, making it harder to understand him, but I enjoyed the effect of a groveling man. "I found him attempting to flee several towns over. He'd let the god get away and was afraid of your repercussions."

I let out a groan of rage. It had been a mistake to send that bumbling fool to watch Lú and make sure he retrieved the Morrigu. But a cleverer man couldn't be trusted. "What has the world come to when an army of grown men can't subdue a goddamn teenager?"

"Begging your pardon, Your Majesty, but he's not just a teen—"

"He's a fallen god, Lynch!" I roared. My strongest predator flinched. "Do you make it a habit of letting impotent spirits of old overpower you?"

"No, Your Majesty."

"Good." I rubbed my temple. Things had gone terribly awry. With the knowledge that Lú had failed to seduce the Morrigu, I'd done what had to be done: I'd unleashed the barbaric multitudes on her. While I'd been confident one of them would turn her in to me, I hadn't bargained on Lú escaping. He may have been a powerless teenager, but if he found a way around the triskele … I didn't need this added complication. "Where have they gone?" I asked Lynch.

"We don't know, Your Majesty. When I got to the castle, it was in ruins."

Movement at the back of the chamber drew my attention. There was stirring inside the great iron cage there. I stood and ambled to it, making sure to take my time and give the man a few moments to come back to consciousness.

"So, Doyle," I said, stepping up to the rusted bars of the cage. "We need to have a bit of a chat, I'm afraid."

He lifted his head just far enough to see me from his spot on the floor. Filthy and weak, he was a poor sight indeed.

"I just need to know one thing: Where have your daughters gotten off to, hmm?" I clasped my hands behind my back. "If you'd just give me a few ideas on where they might go should their home be destroyed, I'd be happy to let you out for a little romp today."

The man stared at me. "Did you destroy it?"

I rolled my eyes. "Come now, Doyle. I don't have all day."

His eyes turned to ice. "Go to hell," he whispered.

"Ah, now." I shook my head. "There's no need to get nasty. It's no matter, truly. We will find them. And you will rot here until the end of time."

Giving him a tight smile, I turned on my heel and marched back to my throne. "Go find them, Lynch!" I barked at my finest hunter. "Take every man in my employ and search every inch of Connacht!"

acknowledgments

Huge thanks, as always, to the million people who make each of my books possible. This one is no exception. I never could have made it past draft one without my very first beta reader, Jane. (That's my mom, you guys). And my Irish-language translator, Becca.

A shout out to my sharp-eyed editor, Amy McNulty, and thanks to Renee Harleston for her brilliant analysis of everything from plot to characters to books not yet written. I also want to thank my other wonderful early readers and extend a continual, unending thank you thank you thank you to my ARCangels review team!

Thanks to my dad, for reading an early version of everything I've ever written; my favorite Rottweiler mix, Lucy, for being herself; and last but not least, my own Irish dream guy, who took me to a castle in Ireland this past summer to get married. Dream. Come. True.

about the author

A short, dog-obsessed, ketchup-loving romantic from the middle of the U.S., Annie Cosby spent three years living in Galway, Ireland, which gave her mono, set her soul on fire, and introduced her to her husband.

She is the author of the *USA Today*-recommended *Hearts Out of Water* and *Souls Out of Ireland* series, the Amazon-chart-soaring *Humming Song Saga,* and countless other tales seeped in Celtic lore.

She now lives in St. Louis, Missouri, with a Rottweiler mix named Lucy and her favorite Irishman.

Sign up for her Readers Club and find more bookish fun at AnnieCosby.com.

books by annie cosby

HEARTS OUT OF WATER

All the Tales We Tell

Lifespan of a Memory

The Last Secret

Fadó, Fadó: Selkies, Kelpies and Other Celtic Creatures

(A Companion Collection to Hearts Out of Water)

SOULS OUT OF IRELAND

The Daughters of Morrigan

THE HUMMING SONG SAGA

Daughter of the Diamond King